HIGHMAGE'S PLIGHT

D. H. Aire

To Colleen,

Dare to Believe!

D. H. Aire

Balticon 2017

HIGHMAGE'S PLIGHT

Other books by D.H. Aire

Highmage's Plight Series

Merchants and Mages
Human Mage
Highmage
Well Armed Brides
Prophecies and Paradox*

Dare2Believe Series

Dare2Believe*
Double Dare*

Terran Catalyst Series

Terran Catalyst*

*forthcoming

D.H. AIRE

Highmage's Plight
Copyright © 2012 by D.H. Aire
Cover Copyright © by Christina Yoder
Edited by Andrew Jones
ISBN: 978-1623750381

Publisher's Note: This is a work of fiction. All characters, places, businesses, and incidents are from the author's imagination. Any resemblance to actual places, people, or events is purely coincidental. Any trademarks mentioned herein are not authorized by the trademark owners and do not in any way mean the work is sponsored by or associated with the trademark owners. Any trademarks used are specifically in a descriptive capacity.

Second Printing

Visit us at www.chimerabook.com

HIGHMAGE'S PLIGHT

Prologue

Hooves clomping down the woodland trail, the unicorn raced, as it had too often during its unceasing vigil these past five thousand years. Horn aglow, it called across hundreds of leagues to give warning to the only one left who might foil the Demonlord's madness. Goblins attacked in numbers uncountable as trumpets blew seeking to rally the faltering Imperial legionnaires, many of whom were being dragged down from the walls of their stone border fortresses.

The chorus of trumpets faltered and a final note abruptly ended as its signaler was cut to pieces by goblins howling in glee.

A goblin mage turned and pointed south at the retreating shape of the unicorn, racing toward the kingdom of Gwire and the Imperials border beyond it. "Stop him!"

Scores shoved past their maniacal brethren who still fought the desperate legionnaires in chainmail stained red. Howling, they gave chase to the distant blur of white.

With a backward glance, eyes wide, the unicorn saw his pursuers. Thoughts flickered to when this had all begun so long ago.

The unicorn galloped down the nearest trail, leaping the brush. The trees of the Great Forest screamed as axes smote their bark and dug deep into their wooden hearts.

Two humans paused to heft a longsaw as unseen eyes watched from the dense thicket and the breeze carried the trees cries far and wide.

"They dare?" the elvin prince whispered to his companion.

"All they seem to know is how to destroy," Lord Summer muttered.

"Likely why they crossed the galaxy in that behemoth out there."

The ship that had fallen from the stars lay beached like a great leviathan where it clove the hills for leagues to the east.

"By now earth is a lifeless rock," Lord Summer said.

"I understand the ancestors' decision to leave their world rather than conquer it. But the humans have no right to commit their atrocities on this world...our world!"

"The tales of the humans warned they would treat their world like this. The king will have to take action now."

They winced at the sound of a tree falling to the earth. "It will not be easy," Summer said glancing at the unicorn that had silently joined their vigil.

The stallion shook its head, horn aglow. Across the heartland of the People, the Guardian of the Gate saw through the unicorn's eyes. Thousands of humans were building settlements and now encroaching on lands that they would never possess.

Something large and silver shot across the sky. Humanity was not as the elves remembered. They had tricks, created light, machines that built structures and mined the earth of metals. Above the elvin lords a falc soared, watching, no more pleased by the humans' actions than they.

"My father cannot but wage war on them now."

Lord Summer nodded, "Aye, my prince."

Years passed. The unicorn's hooves clomped down a burned and rutted trail as the last stallion left the ruined lands laid waste after battles unremitting in the war most terrible. Refugees struggled onward. Those too weak to survive lay dead of starvation or pestilence. Elvin curses marked not a few of the faltering humans. No silver sky runners challenged the horizon any longer. No weapons of light or black powder smote the mageborn or their kindred, which had killed thousands of brave warriors and their helpless kin when they were driven from their homes in the trees and burrows beneath the earth.

The Great Forest, which the elves had sought to save, was no more, ravaged in the flames of hatred, a hatred that had driven the Elfking beyond madness.

An old woman urged a dozen orphaned children to their feet then saw the unicorn observing them, seemingly appearing from nothing.

"Well, you could help, you know."

The unicorn blinked, towering above the woman.

"Miz Estha!"

The old scientist ignored the child's shout, knowing they had the most to fear having lost so much. But she could care less. The worst had already happened.

"Oh, don't give me that," she rasped at the mythical creature as the refugees looked about anxious and afraid. "Name's Estha McQuin, I suppose I'm the de facto leader around here."

The stallion's horn glowed and distant eyes now looked through its gaze.

"Grandmother!" her granddaughter Anniya cried, running up from a group of injured she'd been trying to help to no avail.

"Oh, hush, dear. We're only having an impromptu parley."

Anniya stared but came no closer as the old woman raised her hand and stroked the white unicorn's soft face.

The unicorn snorted. "See? We mean you no harm. Look, we're starving. We're no threat to you or your friends anymore. Anyway, your magic has won the war, making most of our scientific laws moot. So, let's leave the stupidity behind. We could use your help."

The unicorn's horn glowed and his eyes suddenly glittered, glancing at the thousands who had traveled so far yet were still far from safety.

You must head west and south, a deep melodic voice said in her mind.

"West and south?" the old woman muttered. "And your people?"

The Guardian paused, looking out through the eyes of the unicorn, knowing his people had suffered as greatly as this remnant of humanity. "North where the Forest still thrives."

"We need food, water."

"West and south. The unicorn shall lead you."

7

"Thank you."

The aged elf stared into the fire so many leagues distant. "You are... welcome."

The Guardian looked up from the mageborn fire, the unicorn seeing through him. He rose, calling representatives of the remaining Great Houses. They gathered, looking drawn and haggard.

A scarred veteran glared, "Look at us. We all know the truth. We all feel it! I, for one, didn't fight only to die bled to death of spirit by what once my king!"

That set off the debate on what must be done.

The Elfking, in his madness, was calling magery about him, cackling and demented, dark and bitter, colder than winter. "I shall eradicate every last one of the vermin! Every last one for what they have done! I shall feast on them all! Feast!"

The ranting echoed across the winds carried from the leafless trees stripped of life by the mad king's spells.

"We have a choice," the Guardian told the assemblage as the People, young and old, cringed. "Give in to the madness and give up our last shreds of a soul or walk a new path, one with the humans."

They argued, seeking some other way to avert disaster.

"The demon possessing our king is too powerful!" one elf lord shouted.

"We gave him our oaths!" another cried.

"We swore to the Elfking, not to that thing!" a mother, clutching her young child yelled.

"He will destroy us all with the powers he raises!" others chorused.

The Guardian nodded, "We have one hope, if we stand together."

They looked at each other and made decisions that sealed their fate. The assemblage grew smaller as the Guardian called to the Gate.

Time seemed to pass in the blink of an eye as the Gate responded to that summons, for the human refugees days passed as

8

they headed west and south led to untainted free flowing rivers and streams, apple-like fruits, berries, and game in abundance. The unicorn rode at the head of the refugee column with Estha McQuin and her granddaughter upon his back, directing the remnant of humanity.

The unicorn paused as storm clouds massed in the north. Its horn suddenly blazed with brilliant light. Neighing, it bowed to the earth, allowing the two women slide off its flanks.

"We come!" the Guardian cried.

The humans knew not what was happening as the winds of magery began to reach southward. Darkness ripped reality as the Gate opened, and scores of elves appeared from its midst, fleeing their former king's madness.

The refugees trembled and drew back.

"Ward!" the first through shouted as his kindred raced to establish a perimeter, setting a defense they feared would do little good against the forces raised.

The demon's laughter echoed across the growing wind. Then the Guardian stepped through, knowing no others were coming to join them, knowing their decision meant their doom.

His silver hair blowing wildly behind him, he shouted in elvin, raising the full power of the Gate against the raging winds that knocked the humans from their feet, which was only the wave front for what was to come. The rippling darkness twisted about, bending reality as it rose into the sky to meet the evils threatening them all.

And so the new age began in a battle of magery with the survival of humanity and the traitorous elves that had abandoned their mad liege at stake. It was a battle neither side won as the Guardian called up the Gate. It burst forth above them in the sky swallowed the roiling winds of the demon wrought life stealing magery cast by their once great king far to the north.

The clouds parted as the unicorn reared, sunlight bathing him. Estha McQuin rose, dusting herself off and shouting at her granddaughter and their people, "Well, you lot, show some hospitality to our friends! They look worse for wear than we do!"

The unicorn had watched as the goblins, descendants of the elves who had, out of fear, remained loyal to the twisted demonic shadow of the Elfking. They broke through the Imperial mages' wards as they had too often over the centuries, but this time as the legionnaires fought to turn them back something was amiss.

"Reinforcements!" a commander cried.

None came.

Scryers shouted, "We've lost our link!"

Goblins screamed, cutting down the legionnaires and their mages defending the borderlands.

The unicorn reared and called a warning that echoed through the ether that reached the latest Guardian of the Gate in his study, at the very heart of the Empire.

The stallion raced south, its goblins pursuers bounding ever closer. He had to see what other mischief the Demonlord had managed, that he might relay it as the Highmage hurried to sit before his fireplace to establish a full mental link, afraid of what he was to learn.

Chapter 1: Highmage's Plight

Flames crackled in the fireplace, the room's only source of light set along the center of the stone wall. Shadows were cast over the intricately carved thousand-year-old desk and stacks of books on Imperial history and magery piled high in every corner. The aged, silver haired Highmage sat facing the fire chanting a spell. The flames gyrated higher with every word and an image formed.

He felt the call from the Northlands to seek vision from the fire. The unicorn reared within the flames. Through the unicorn's eyes, he could see Imperial troops fleeing before a horde of goblins. The kingdom of Gwire, for long centuries the Empire's ally, had to have fallen by treason, allowing the Demonlord's armies to wreak havoc there. The Highmage sighed, seeing smoke rising from the ruins of the overrun line of border fortresses. Goblins could be seen flowing out of it, the blood of their victims drenching their weapons and mail.

Thunder pealed outside, which shook the Highmage clear of the vision. As rain poured on the tile roof, he could hear the Demonlord's laughter in that thunder. It had begun! The Age of Mankind upon the face of this world was drawing to a close.

Trembling, the Highmage, the Guardian of this world, knew that with the northern forces in disarray it would only be a matter of time before the Empire itself fell. Ancient prophecy held that should Gwire and its Royal House fall, the Demonlord's victory was assured. So the Empire had pledged troops to forever defend the borderlands.

With a wave of his hand, he felt the unicorn racing south. Time past seemingly in moments and the image in the fire showed the King of Gwire struck down, the heir fallen as he struggled to rally the city guard and his household troops.

There must be some remaining shred of hope, the Highmage thought as he added a new note to his chant. The flames crackled and he heard the sound of hooves. There, the unicorn, galloping across the fiery image. The unicorn abruptly halted to stare back at the Highmage. He nodded at the creature, knowing it was the last of its kind. The unicorn's horn glowed with power, disrupting the enchanted flames, raising up another image, deep within the ethereal flames. .

The unicorn presented a vision of a carriage riding up the streets of the Imperial Capital, this very city. It was under the escort of scores of mounted black liveried warriors. The sight puzzled the aged Highmage. He realized that he was looking at a people mentioned only in stories told by sailors, or referred to only in journals and history books. Cathartans, legendary for their sword skill, they dwelled in lands far beyond the Empire's borders, far to the southeast, beyond even the Barrier Mountains and south of the Great Waste. What made their presence far more unusual was the fact that they were cursed, and so rarely, if ever, left their land.

The Highmage wondered what they were doing there as they vanished in a flash of lightning. The storm outside raged where the unicorn's vision had placed the Cathartans. When lightning next flashed, they and their carriage appeared again, but slightly farther up the street and in clear weather. The Highmage wondered if this was a vision of things to come.

Aboard the carriage was a brightly cloaked man who cradled a sick boy in his lap. The city around the Cathartan phantoms seemed subtly different. The buildings seemed taller, their façades somehow brighter to the Highmage. Lightning flashed and they were gone once more.

The thunder echoed with the Demonlord's maniacal laughter. Lightning flared again and the phantoms returned, yet the accompanying sound of thunder carried a more muted note of his nemesis' triumph.

What does it mean? Why would the unicorn wish to show me this, the Highmage wondered.

He recalled there had once been a prophecy about Cathart, a land settled by refugees not unlike those who had founded the Empire, except that they were cursed. Few Imperial ships traded there for fear of that curse. The prophecy offered them hope, and he understood the power of that which was not unlike magic. The group faded in and out of existence, and headed up through the Seven Tiered City.

Thunder raged, shaking the capital city of the Empire. Aaprin, an elfblooded apprentice, an adolescent of mixed parentage struggled to see through the heavy rain as he walked, accompanying his elvin master, who repelled the rain from himself with a spell. Aaprin's master used him as a personal errand boy, knowing that the elfblood youth had not a lick of mage talent. Yet his loyalty more than made up for it.

Aaprin grimaced as he saw a strange carriage under heavy escort, heading toward them. The narrow street was not wide enough for two parties. The carriage rode toward them in cloudless sunshine. Aaprin wiped the rain from his eyes in astonishment. His master seemed unconcerned as they crossed in front he could see them no more.

"Master," Aaprin said, "Where did they go?"

"What are you talking about, boy?"

Lightning struck once more. Aaprin shouted in warning as black liveried riders suddenly bore down on them, the sound of their hooves and squeaking carriage wheels rushing forward about to run them down. He dragged his master aside as the coach narrowly missed them.

"Aaprin, what's come over you, lad!" his master cried shaking his arm. "Have you gone mad?"

"Master, whatever are Cathartans doing so far from their southern climes?"

"What are you talking about? No one has ever seen Cathartans in the Empire. Now explain why you pulled me along on such an insane dash!"

He stared uncertainly. "Master, we would have been run down by the horses, otherwise."

With a groan his master shouted, "Aaprin, go back to the Academy this instant! Forget our errand, I shall accomplish it alone! And think hard about your behavior before we next talk about this!"

The young elfblood swallowed and considered protesting, but thought better of it as the last of the foreign women in black livery riding in escort turned down the next street. There could be only one destination along that route. "My pardon, Master Stenh, I will go back this instant."

Huffing, the elvin mage continued up the street while Aaprin ran back the way they came, running after the phantom Cathartans toward the Healers Hall.

There was a knock at the door and a servant answered. "Lord Stenh! What brings you out on such a terrible night?"

As the servant took his cloak, Stenh asked, "Is the Highmage about?"

"Yes, but he has asked to be left alone."

"I must see him. The matter is urgent."

The Highmage's elvin daughter appeared at the top of the stairs, "Take Master Stenh to my father."

The mage looked up at her, gratefully.

"He has been in his study since his meeting with the Empress."

He nodded in understanding and said, "Thank you, Carwina."

Stenh was led into the Highmage's study. The aged elf sat humming to himself and was hunched forward looking into the flames in his fireplace. The servant closed the door firmly behind him as Stenh waited patiently, knowing the Highmage was in the midst of a powerful spell. The mage sighed, thinking the Highmage must already know the terrible truth.

The Highmage's chant grew more intense and the flames before him rose higher as he leaned forward. He saw an image form that resembled a space in the capital. The healers came forth and offered to assist with the Cathartan boy. The women refused as a darkly dressed man led them into the building. The image shifted as Master Healer Ofran, himself, took charge of the seriously ill child. He saw the old elf frown after examining the lad and could see his lips form the words, "I can ease his pain, but nothing more."

The Cathartan lord's shoulders slumped.

14

The Highmage frowned and gave up the chant. The flames flickered to normalcy.

"Alrex," Stenh muttered behind him.

The Highmage sighed. "I had hoped to be left undisturbed on a night as terrible as this, my friend."

"I am sorry, Alrex, but the news I bring is dire; the Academy scryers saw a glimpse of the Northlands. They are lost. Gwire has fallen," Stenh told him with a shiver. "The Imperial Legion there has been cut off from all support."

"I know."

"The Empress will be forced to send additional troops. There will be war…the Final War."

"There will be no reinforcements. The Demonlord's minions work unseen. The Empress will not engage the remainder of the Legions until assured that they will not be thrown away in vain, fearing the end has, indeed, come. The true stakes of the Final War hinge upon what happens next."

"But the Empress must!"

The Highmage laughed forlornly. "I have spoken to her. She believes our combined magery still leaves us evenly matched enough that we have time."

Stenh, Dean of the Mage Academy, shook his head, "But we both know we no longer command the power our people once did. Only your mastery of the Gate as Guardian offers us any hope."

Alrex lowered his head. He knew the Gate's limitations all too well.

"Leave me."

As Master Stenh went through the door, Carwina whispered to him and gestured down the hall. She entered and said, "Father, I have given Stenh a room for the night. I'll not have him hazard the storm once more."

He shook his head, "Your healer training has made you too kind, Carwina."

"And you need to sleep and leave off worrying about the fate of humanity. I would be happy to bring you a draught."

"You were listening."

She shrugged, "I was. Nothing else would have brought him across the city unescorted. It had to have been worth listening to."

"You are a trying child, Carwina."

"I am my father's daughter," she smiled warmly. "And you should leave off worrying about the Demonlord's latest schemes. We can still defeat him."

The Highmage gazed at his daughter in her optimism. "Would that we could." He hugged his robe closer. "The Aqwaine Empire is not the power it once was."

"Yet, the power of the Gate you wield is no small thing."

"So our Empress and the Mage Guild believe but the Gate is not like other mageries. It can only be used in certain ways."

"Still, humanity, even without magery, nearly defeated Elfdom before Battle's End."

"Yes, but they exhausted their 'technology,'" Alrex said, pronouncing the word with great difficulty. "They were forced to flee the lands we together laid waste. Left primitive and hurt, they could offer us no further harm."

"'And from such the Empire was born,'" Carwina quoted from the Chronicles.

Alrex frowned thoughtfully, "Elves and mankind united to create the Empire, setting aside our hatred. But the Elfking's hate was too great… and so he rages against us, now the Lord of Demons."

Thunder shook the mansion. Carwina shivered and hurriedly left her father to his thoughts.

"There must be a way!" Highmage Alrex shouted. He cried a word of power and waved his hand at the stone wall behind him. The stones rippled with magelight, obeying him as the Guardian. Alrex marched across the room and strode through the glowing passage.

He entered the etherworld, a place outside of normal space and time, the antechamber before the Gate. The Highmage stepped forward and reached the Gate, an arch, glowing with raised elvish runes intricately carved by magefire aeons ago. Within the arch's

16

depths stars dimly glowed and illuminated the archway in dull white light.

He knelt before the Gate and humbly lamented, "Our magery is nothing as to what it once was. The Empire crumbles around us more each day. We are no match for what the Demonlord has raised."

The Highmage considered the vision in the flames that had showed him a phantom present. It could be nothing else. Somehow he stood at a crux, a moment of paradox; however, he did not know if the vision was a harbinger of a futile ending for his people. It seemed to promise more time, perhaps hope. "This world needs our help, old friend."

The Gate began to blaze as it awoke fully and considered its Guardian.

For millennia, the Gate between worlds had been closed. Long ago the stars were easily crossed by the Elves, worlds under many suns were called home. Yet, through time, various worlds had been abandoned and their Gates sealed.

The Master Gate in the Highmage's world still thrived but stood alone, as alone as its Elvin Guardian felt this day. For more than two hundred years Alrex had served as Highmage of the Aqwaine Empire. He would likely be the last before the Demonlord, once Elfking, conquered the Empire and in his madness exterminated humanity. Even Carwina believed the Gate could succor them from that fate.

Highmage Alrex knelt for seemingly hours before the Gate, appealing. "…but none of them understand your limits. You are a thing of pure magery. We cannot wield you like a sword. You are a doorway. And, whether they understand it or not, you are alive."

The Gate watched him, understood him, knew the true thoughts of its companion, his fears and sorrows. They were one, Guardian and Gate.

The Gate then did what it had not done for thousands of years. Alrex shielded his eyes as the Gate's runes flared brighter than a sun, reaching out to the beckoning stars of the galaxy.

17

Chapter 2: The Dig

The dig team had uncovered most of the nearby hills and archeologists had staked out their finds. George frowned, leaning on his staff.

"This just doesn't make sense," George muttered to himself. He glanced across the dig and shouted to his graduate student, "Jamie, be careful over there! That equipment is delicate!"

"Sorry, Professor!" the young man yelled back.

George, nearly forty, sighed and privately wished his student assistants were not quite so young. He stepped down into the dig, reaching a depth indicative of a time of more than seven thousand years in the past. The staff in his hand was the newest DHR model, the latest in Data Humanistic Rapport, made of reinforced molicirc computer crystal. It glowed as he entered rapport and muttered to himself, "Initiate scan of the next section."

'Acknowledged,' the computer replied in his mind. George closed his eyes and internally heard it state, *'Initiating scan.'*

The catalogued remains of the structure, the geological formation, the very shape of the dirt and rock were instantly reorganized in his mind's eye. The dig vanished around him. This valley in northern Europe all too suddenly held a series of buildings that were centered around George's location.

A mental blueprint of the city formed as he turned his head, with eyes closed. He visualized each building, some six stories tall, with arched windows and doorways. He had the impression of gigantic interwoven tree trunks and beautifully interlaced branches forming platforms and walkways.

The stones that formed the walls had been intricately carved with symbols reminiscent of runes, but not recognized ones. The roofs were inclined, supported by thick wooden beams. Groves of trees had been planted around each structure, almost concealing the town.

The high level of expertise this demonstrated is what confused him most. This should have been a primitive age. However, the technology used to build these structures seemed far too advanced.

His peers ridiculed his findings, and the university began questioning the entire project in light of his seemingly contradictory discoveries. This place should not have existed; humanity should not have had the skill to build these particular structures, yet the evidence was before him. Later in the day he would have the opportunity, if one could call it that, to present his findings to a team from the university, fellow experts in the history of this area who were charged with assessing the academic merit of George's controversial work. DHR enhanced archaeology was often considered a subjective science, since it depended on the archaeologist's perception and experience, which made this find suspect in the closed minds of his many rather conservative peers.

He felt it was so damned frustrating. The technology was invaluable; however, after thousands of years, new finds of this type were extremely rare. The support of the university was essential to making his making his mark on the historical record, even if it might go against everything they knew of human history of this place and time.

The entire length of the computer staff glowed as George walked within the central building. He could see arches rising majestically up to the ceiling, supporting successive stories. Each block of the stone foundation had been precisely cut and set without mortar, which would have left some residue. The stone floor had been polished as smooth as glass.

George walked deeper into the imagined structure and looked about him, trying to ascertain its purpose. He paused and closed his eyes again, wondering if this had been a meeting place or temple of some kind. He opened his eyes, moved to the left, and closed his eyes to observe the site he was exploring with his staff from a new vantage.

There were a number of archways off to one side. One arch led to stairs that spiraled upward to the higher floors. All led to chambers, which served no immediately obvious purpose. There was also no evidence that this had been a burial tomb, but the greatest oddity was across the main chamber. An archway fronted the thick exterior wall, serving no structural need. Perhaps he was still missing some vital piece of data that would provide a further clue, or even answer to why it was there.

'Anomaly detected.'

That was curious. When their equipment had first uncovered this level, there had been no anomalous readings. He reached the unusual archway and knelt to examine the two remaining base stones. "Split vision, please," he muttered.

'Acknowledged.'

He saw both the projections of the arch and the base stone that was its only remnant. Kneeling closer, he unclipped a stiff brush from his belt and used it to clear another layer of dirt. Exposing the stone further, he frowned.

"Identify the base rock."

The staff glowed for a moment.

'Unable to comply. No identifiable trace elements detected. Negative identification of substances of terrestrial origin.'

"Could it have come from meteoritic material?"

'No radiation detected, unable to provide complete evaluation to advance a hypothesis.' George glanced at the projected arch, more curious than ever as to its purpose and origins.

"Professor Bradley!" Jamie shouted. "The Archive's team has arrived!"

Great, he thought aggrieved, they're early.

He rose, preoccupied with the mysterious archway.

"Professor Bradley!" Jamie shouted, smiling crookedly at the assembled university team members and added, "Right this way, ladies and gentlemen."

The team looked less than pleased.

"I'm coming!" George shouted back, realizing he had lost track of time, the staff still glowing enrapport with his mind.

George began to turn away, excited by the find, his mind still partially envisioning the mysterious archway.

"Professor!" Jamie shouted, glancing down the edge of the excavation with the curious archival team.

At the base of the dig, George's glowing computer staff faintly touched the revealed base of one of the ancient, unidentifiable stones. There was a sudden blast, an indescribable sound. Energy arced between the two stones before George could see what caused it.

Wind howled behind him as he found himself paralyzed, unable to move, and uncertain of what was happening.

The Highmage gaped as he saw sudden light amid the brightening stars within the Gate. Incredibly, a distant Gate opened. Alrex jerked to his feet and yelled the Invocation of Entry. The runes flared the length of the Gate as it lowered its veil and opened to the cosmos.

A scaled claw was outthrust from the other side of the Gate and raked the unprepared Highmage. He screamed in agony as he fell backward, clutching his bloody chest. A hulking gray scaled wyvern, its sharp teeth barred, leapt through the portal and into the ethereal antechamber, landing on its four heavily taloned feet.

"Kill him, my pet!" the Demonlord shouted from the other side.

The Highmage mumbled a word of power and a bolt of fire shot from his curled, blood smeared fingertips. The wyvern was flung aside with a cry. Alrex reached out and grasped at one of the arch's flaring runes.

He shouted a desperate command even as his eyes widened, seeing what looked like a shooting star fall across the Heavens. The Gate sealed shut, its runes fading to darkness. The wyvern screamed as the wards set about this place trapped it, momentarily keeping it at bay.

Alrex struggled to his feet and flung himself past the snorting wyvern, and out of limbo. It glared at him, struggling to move as he passed back into his study.

The Highmage abruptly fell gasping to the floor as the wall behind him began to solidify. The wyvern roared suddenly free of the wards and leapt after him. Alrex turned on his side and watched the wall return to solid stone around the wyvern's head and one outstretched leg. The creature's eyes glazed with death, its head and limb jutting forth from the wall like some hunter's prize.

Alrex lay panting, pale, and dazed.

Aaprin followed the phantom Cathartans to the Healers Hall, where the storm kicked up into even greater fury. Wind tore at him as he raced past the huddled phantoms and their carriage inside the courtyard, who were unaffected by the storm raging about Aaprin while they stood in calm daylight.

The young apprentice mage thrust open the hall door and shoved it closed behind him. The duty warden shouted at the soaking wet apprentice for his foolishness.

"The matter that brought you here had better be urgent, boy!"

Aaprin gaped as the Cathartans solidified and the warden faded as would a phantom. The whole Hall had taken on a surreal look. Everything around him seeming to glare, suddenly blinding him. He shook his head in disbelief, blinked several times, and stared at the solidifying image of the Master Healer Ofran, addressing the Cathartan lord.

His lips moved and at first, Aaprin heard no sound. Then came the words, "I can ease his pain, but nothing more."

"We've traveled so far. Is there truly no magery that can save him?" the man pleaded.

Suddenly Aaprin felt a hand come down on his shoulder. He looked up, startled almost as much as the black liveried woman next to him. "Where did you come from?" she asked.

"Me'oh, get him out of here!" another ordered, ushering him forcefully out and muttering, "Blasted elvin magery."

Aaprin looked about him, feeling dizzy and unsure as to why. "Ignore, Cle'or, she takes her duty a bit too seriously. Best be off before she considers you a real threat," Me'oh commented.

"Uh, sorry, I didn't mean to disturb anyone."

Or had he, he wondered. *What was he doing here?* He shook his head seeing the black liveried women and her companions, armed with short swords and daggers, standing guard throughout the anteroom. They watched him warily.

"Me'oh, how did he get in here?" one of her blonde-haired companions asked.

She propelled him past her sisters. "That's simple, Se'and; by magery, of course." The other black liveried women glared at Aaprin.

"Something that apparently involved a water spell," the youngest woman remarked, frowning at the water dripping from his clothes onto the floor.

The sisters laughed as he quickly exited the hall. Me'oh closed the door firmly behind him as he looked down at himself and realized he was soaking wet.

When did this happen? he wondered.

Standing outside in the courtyard, he paused and glanced up at the clear sky. Vaguely, he remembered a storm but was uncertain when he patted his chest and felt he was completely dry. He shivered and hurriedly returned to the Academy.

The young woman, Fri'il, glanced out the window and watched the elfblood youth run off. She blinked and shook her head. *Why ever did I think he had been soaking wet?*

The howling wind and darkness took George from his place at the dig. He was falling and desperately held tight his staff. As he fell, the crystal glowed brighter and brighter. Still enrapport with the computer, he had the sense of falling forever, past stars, even past planetary masses.

Abruptly the fall ceased and he found himself off his feet, suspended in stygian nothingness, a limbo. He slowly stood erect in midair, struggling to regain his sense of balance. Only the brilliant light from his crystalline staff allowed him to see at all. That light revealed, out of the depths of the darkness, two rather large hunched slit nosed, scaled creatures with luridly glowing eyes.

They leapt at George, who swung the glowing staff to fend them off. They shrieked in pain, shying away from the light, then charged as the light receded. George struck one on the side of its belly as it neared, at the impact: smoke and searing. The creature hastily fell back with a cry. They were not long deterred, and returned to their attack. Their powerful teeth gnashed at him as he beat them back. They swiped their horrible talon-like claws at him as he ducked aside. One of the beasts finally broke past George's guard and tried to disembowel him.

The staff flared to even brighter intensity as he hastily struck out to block the sweeping talons. The glowing staff connected with but a glancing blow, yet at the touch there was a resounding burst and the creature shriveled as the light danced about its skin.

The next beast raked George's exposed flank with a powerful swipe of its claws. He screamed in agony, twisting to defend himself from further attack. The creature's fiery eyes gleamed in delight even as the ground seemed to suddenly give way beneath them.

George fell once more through eternity. He clutched his computer staff for dear life as it flared with light like a beacon across a stormy night. Then, out of the darkness, George struck the ground hard, losing his grip on his staff at last. His only impression before he lost consciousness was of ghastly shocked faces surrounding him, edged by firelight.

Carwina awoke from the strangest dream, which was already beginning to fade from memory. She had seen Gwire falling, the last days nearly upon its people. She shook her head, knowing it was only a bad dream, as she heard her father cry out in agony. She raced to her father's study and saw light from under the door. She entered and cried "Father!" in sudden horror.

She hurried to her father who lay bleeding on the floor. She recoiled at the sight of the wyvern's dismembered head and leg on the wall, locked in its moment of death. The servants heard her and rushed upstairs. They stared aghast at the wyvern as Carwina shouted, "Summon Master Ofran!"

She summoned her own courage and began a healing chant for her father.

At the courtyard, the Cathartan lord, Sire Ryff, was led to a cot. He sat dejected as his Mother Shaman took her place beside him and hugged him.

"It was all for naught, De'ohr," he lamented.

"No, Ryff, it was not," she whispered.

"The prophecy brought us here. It's been the only hope I've had to cling to. Yet to learn that they can provide no help at all?"

The woman shook her head. "I cannot explain it. The prophecy was quite explicit. 'When the secondson descended of the Shattered House falls to the Curse, to the Empire its lord must take him, else succor of House and world fall with him.' Here is where I foresaw we must come if there was to be any hope. Destiny demanded our presence here, at this very moment. We are here for a reason, Ryff, and as long as your son still lives, there is hope of healing him."

Tears misted his eyes. "You are truly crazed. I, too, must be to cling to such a forlorn hope."

"The Curse warps our whole nation, Ryff. Today there are only thirty-six men in all of Cathart. The first secondson in generations is a great blessing. We cannot afford to lose him. I feel the current of fate. Our trek here has not been in vain."

"What would you have me do now?"

"Rest. Accept what help the Master Healer offers young Vyss. After that, we shall see. Events will make matters clear."

Chapter 3: Ruins

Ashra Kodiu, once seat of Elvin power, now lay a ruin in the Great Waste. The dozen hunters of Prect had scouted before Greth was certain enough that the goblins had actually migrated north. Ashra Kodiu was a prize they could rarely hunt.

They scavenged during the daylight hours then retreated into one of the least damaged structures in the exact center of the city. It seemed safe enough, so Greth permitted them the luxury of a fire. The chamber was high ceilinged and well screened from outside observation. One never knew when goblins were about.

The hunt had gone well. They had found several old elvin swords, some shields and armor, and, most importantly, enchanted jewels. The best had been discovered in a bespelled cache deep in the warrens. Finding the cache alone had made their mission worthwhile; especially, since it would likely be a long time before they ever got another chance to raid there.

Greth gripped his sword hilt and rose before his men.

"Tomorrow we will continue the Hunt. But I want the watch doubled! The goblins covet this city and are likely to have left a few surprises for us!"

The others nodded. Prudence was a necessary quality in successful hunters and openly engaging goblins and others of their ilk was not the best strategy, not if they wished to see their home of Prect again any time soon.

The fire burned low as Greth slept after his watch. He was awakened by a frigid breeze as the guard on duty shouted a warning and pointed toward the far wall. An arched alcove was glowing and wind now began to whistle forth.

Pulling his sword from its sheath, Greth readied himself, fearing he had made a terrible error in choosing this place to rest. A figure was propelled out of the absolute darkness of the elvin gateway and fell hard on the stone floor.

The chamber was momentarily bright with light from the staff that the intruder clutched in his hand, which slowly tumbled out of reach. Greth and his hunters gathered and stared in wonder at what the sudden intense light had revealed. It was a man.

There was a terrifying roar and something else bounded from the gateway. At the mere sound of it, Greth yelled and charged. The sword's touch raised smoke on the creature's scaled but leathery hide. It shrieked at the presence of the bane metal.

The hunters' blades were all of the same discolored alloy that elvinkind abhorred. The wyvern roared once more as it found itself under attack on all sides. It struck and one of Greth's fellows was knocked aside.

Another quickly took his place as the beast leapt over them, trying to get at its unconscious target, the man from the Gate. Greth slammed his sword upward. With a scream, the wyvern fell short of the man and the hunters hurried to block its path.

The fight raged on and on. A second, then third hunter fell back, clutching injuries as Greth began to gasp for breath. Pulling out his knife, Greth leapt upon the wyvern's back. It bucked as he edged forward and thrust his dagger into the hilt into the wyvern's skull.

It shrieked in pain, staggered a step, then seemed to gain strength. To Greth's surprise, it would not die. The beast knocked Greth off its back, its eyes blazing with unholy fire as it ignored Greth and his fellows, focusing exclusively on its fallen prey from the ether of the Gate.

The staff glowed ever so faintly from where it lay, just centimeters from the unconscious man's out-flung hand. It quivered as the wyvern stumbled forward, closing on its target. The staff rolled across the ground and came to rest against the man's fingertips.

The staff flared and a charge like lightning arched to the wyvern's wounded skull. With a shrill scream of agony, the wyvern convulsed and fell dead. Smoke rose from the body as the staff's glow diminished. There was a startled silence for a moment then groans as Greth and his companions slowly rose to their feet.

"Is everyone all right?" Greth asked.

His men acknowledged him then looked incredulously at the injured man and his now quiescent staff.

Carwina stood over her injured father.

"I'm fine," Alrex muttered weakly as a blue flame played across the gaping wound at his side.

Carwina, visibly perspiring from the exertion of maintaining the healing chant, was preventing further blood loss.

Master Ofran replied, "No, you are not," and directed a concerned look at Stenh.

The Highmage rasped, "You do not understand…. I have no time for this."

Stenh frowned, "Can you tell us what happened?"

"No time for this… There are things I must do," groaned the Highmage.

"The only thing you must do, my friend, is rest," Ofran advised, knowing that the injury was grave. Wyvern borne wounds were notoriously difficult to heal. Many faced a painful lingering death from such wounds.

"Gwire is safe," Alrex whispered. "I can feel it."

Stenh frowned, "What are you talking about? Of course Gwire's safe. The legions are allied with the Rangers, after all. The Northland border is well defended."

Alrex blinked in surprise, "Rangers?"

Stenh looked at the healer, "Can you help him?"

"I could do more at the Healers Hall."

The mage shook his head, "Any rumor of the Highmage being incapacitated must not be allowed to leak! It could set off a panic!"

Alrex lay back and frowned, "Rangers…"

Ofran frowned, "Stenh, I must fetch my colleagues downstairs."

Alrex coughed, "No need. I know what must be done. The Demonlord will be livid, realizing what I have wrought." He coughed again, wetly. "His victory is no longer assured."

Stenh gestured for Ofran to stay and rushed to send up the other healers, faintly hearing the Highmage say, "I must live long enough to see this through."

"Alrex?" Ofran muttered. He heard the Highmage begin to chant.

Carwina abruptly stopped her chanting and gasped, "Father, please! Please, do not do this!"

"What is happening?" Stenh asked as he returned from calling the healers. Behind them ran his kind-hearted, but rather useless apprentice, Aaprin.

Alrex's chanted spell came to a whisper.

"Father," Carwina begged. "Please, don't."

"Alrex, give us a chance to heal these wounds!" Ofran pleaded.

"Please, Father, let us help you!"

Two young healers had taken up the chanting, leaving Master Healer Ofran to try to stop what Alrex had put in motion.

It was too late. The spell was complete. Alrex took a deep breath.

"I am the Guardian," he rasped. "I am too old to battle as I must. My death must not be a victory for the Demonlord."

"Father," Carwina cried.

He smiled at her. "I do what I must," then he opened his hand, revealing an ancient stone rune. The rune had an embossed image of a rearing unicorn. It pulsed with darkness that welled outward over his palm, wrapping around him.

The healers ceased their chanting and retreated.

"Speak with the Empress…" Alrex muttered. "The Gate shall hold my death at bay, allowing me the time I need to impart gifts that shall assuredly be to the Demonlord's rue."

Tears flowed over Carwina's cheeks as the darkness seethed and covered her father. He vanished within an opaque cocoon.

A piece of the Highmage's spirit fled from his enchanted body. It left the capital and flew free, heading eastward. It quickly left the

Empire, crossed the clouds that hung above the Crescent Lands, and as the morning sun rose it came to the Barrier Mountains.

As it ascended over the peaks an elderly man looked up from his tent and gasped. The spirit hardly paused, tasting a comforting presence unfelt in many years.

I seek him. Must seek him. He must come. Must!

"Alrex, what have you done?" the old man whispered as that bit of spirit sped past and descended into the Great Waste, seeking, searching amidst the desolation, where nothing of humanity or elvinkind should survive.

None of the hunters had been able to touch the glowing staff. Each time one tried, they had been burned. Finally, Greth hit upon an idea. He skinned the wyvern's side of its magical hide and draped it over the staff, wrapping it.

"We must hurry. The Demonlord will summon his minions here."

The hunters dressed the unconscious man's wounds then carried him away from Ashra Kodiu. Many of them were bandaged, yet held close their prizes. Greth carried the staff, which gave off not the faintest bit of light now. The wyvern hide seemed to shape itself around the crystal form. Soon, the staff began to appear as if merely wood. The hunters looked at him with worry.

"It is all right. Wyverns are masters at disguising themselves with their surroundings. Now we know their secret."

Something unseen arrowed across the terrain. Greth felt it as a breeze that suddenly swirled around him.

The man from the Gate groaned as it struck him full force. The hunters watched him closely, wondering if the man was waking. But he remained unconscious as they quickly trekked home.

In a dream, George fell through the void and screamed, "What's happening to me?!"

A voice answered, *You will come.*

An image arose of a strange multi-tiered city with high defensive stone walls.

Come you must!

Darkness shrouded the image as a voice shouted across the depths of the overwhelming blackness.

"Find him! Destroy him or all my plans will be in ruins!"

The other voice whispered softly, *You will come. Answers you shall have. You are the cusp of paradox and the only hope for my world.*

George physically shook, feeling as if part of him had been ripped in half. "What's happening to me?"

This time there was no answer.

Chapter 4: The Waste

Casber sat at the cliff's edge, his favorite perch. The Barrier Mountains stretched north and south for as far as could be seen. Below him was the Great Waste, seemingly an endless desert. He daydreamed about the times of legend, when the barren land had been the cradle of human civilization, destroyed in the ancient war between man and elves.

The Waste conjured images of magical forces in conflagration. Weapons devised by the lost and forgotten humans had been wielded to devastating effect. The result was the barren land before him.

He sighed, surveying the land of his fancy as the sun settled lower. Fire raged and great beasts fought long forgotten heroes in his memories. The once lush land had been laid waste and mankind had been forced to flee, seeking green undamaged land in the west beyond the mountain chain where he lived.

With a smile, Casber imagined the ancient struggle. White fire blasted shapes of opacity. The light flashed as the attackers were driven back, only to rush forth once more. The answering blast of light brought with it the sound of thunder.

Casber blinked and his face sullied. He leaned forward, realizing he was seeing real mage fire, not some memory of it. The final rays of daylight dimmed upon the Great Waste and suddenly he saw nothing more.

"Casber!" his brother shouted, jogging up the trail.

The boy quickly rose, pausing to glance once more down at the Waste. He cried, "Did you see that, Niel? Did you?"

"What are you talking about, Cas?"

"Down there! There was a battle!"

"Have you scared yourself silly with your games again? Come on, we're gonna be late for supper!"

"But, but…" he tried to explain as his older brother grabbed his arm and dragged him away.

"Do stop your prattling and don't try telling any tales. Papa's had quite enough of your foolishness. Now come on!"

And so it was with the whole family at supper.

His Uncle Wane laughed, "Magefire and battles in the Waste, indeed!"

"What do you suppose you'll see tomorrow?" his younger cousin, Cort, muttered, glancing at Niel before laughing.

"Probably a dragon," was his brother's reply that carried clear across the serving tent.

That brought universal laughter which rang in Casber's ears. His father glared at him with a glint in his eye that was a promise of summary punishment at his foolishness. Casber sighed, knowing they would not understand. He dreaded the extra duties he was sure to be given.

Then his elfblooded uncle, Balfour, came over and whispered, "Elder Winome wishes to speak with you afterward."

Casber swallowed hard. "Who, me?"

His grandfather, Elder of Clan Winome of the Barrier Mountains, was in the tent he shared with his half-caste unmarried son. Balfour swept the hide covering the doorway aside and ushered his young nephew in.

Casber stood in trepidation before the wizened old man in trepidation. The Elder ruled the Clan with but a word. His sons respected his wisdom and authority. Casber had never before been invited alone into his grandfather's presence. Always before he had come with his cousins and siblings to be regaled by the Elder's tales and lessons from his travels across the Crescent Lands and the Empire beyond, but never before had he solely been summoned.

It was the Elder who taught Casber to respect the Great Waste, which most of the Clan ignored as just a fact of life. He, too, had taken the Great Waste for granted until the Elder told them the stories of its history.

"So, grandson, you claim to have seen one of the legendary battles?"

"No, I – uh, I mean that I thought so at first. But only at first," he resigned.

The old man grinned wryly. "Well, why don't you tell me exactly what you think you saw and let me judge."

Casber nervously wringed his fingers. "Might I, uh, sit down first?"

The old man chuckled and gestured, "Please do."

As Casber sat, his grandfather called out, "Balfour!"

His elfblooded uncle glanced back into the tent.

"Yes, father?"

"Do be so kind as to bring us some of that juice. The boy looks parched – I doubt he even ate supper."

"I'll bring another serving as well then."

And with that, Casber found himself once more alone with his grandfather.

"Now, lad, tell me this tale of yours."

Casber swallowed hard and did.

His grandfather listened intently, holding a firm gaze upon the stuttering young elf. As Casber finished his recounting his grandfather exclaimed, "Of course, you must go back in the morning!"

Casber knew his father would not gainsay the order. And his kin would find no more reason to laugh at him!

"You are to report anything you see, but I admonish you to take great care. This is a responsibility to your whole clan! Whatever you saw, whether man, beast, or act of nature, you must report it to me right away, understood?"

The boy nodded, wholeheartedly.

"Now get a good night's sleep and be there at first light!

"Yes, Elder! Thank you, Elder!"

"Have that mother of yours set aside food for your vigil, too!"

Balfour smiled as he saw the lad run out of the tent and across the encampment. He entered the tent and saw his father furrowing his brow. "Don't tell me you believe his tale, Father?"

The old man merely looked back at him with no answer.

Promptly at sunrise, Casber was at his post, looking out over the Great Waste. He waited and watched as the sky grew light. Full morning soon lay across the lowlands as he looked for any sign of movement, anything to support what he saw the day before.

He did not see anything. In frustration, Casber pounded his fists against the rocky outcropping.

"It was there! I didn't imagine it! I know I saw it!" he exclaimed, pounding his fists on the ground.

Stone suddenly shifted, the soil beneath his outcropping perch began to give way. He gasped in horror as the rocky shelf twisted beneath him and slid downward. He cried out and grabbed desperately for a hold as he lost his purchase.

He flailed his arms, screaming, trying to stop plummeting. Rocks cascaded off the cliff face even as a hand reached out for him and pulled him to a halt. Casber momentarily found himself dangling over open air, then felt something brush his mind. He heard a voice.

'Scan complete.'

Casber looked upward. A man held his forearm and muttered something Casber couldn't understand. A dull pain raced through him, then a moment of incredible warmth and peace.

'Language acquired.'

"Hold on!" his rescuer shouted, then drew him up.

Eyes wide, he stared silently at his rescuer, who clung to him with an almost cruel grip. The man's gaze was unfocused. He gasped for breath and relaxed his hold.

"You'll be fine. But I suggest a better choice of perch in the future."

Casber nodded vaguely, staring at the man who had a wooden staff strapped across his back. The man glanced to the right, "That way looks to be the fastest to the top, I think."

"Where did you come from?" Casber asked.

The man ignored his question. "Stick close, young man." They ascended the mountain path.

Casber's mind raced with questions. He stopped and asked, "You climbed the mountain from the Waste, didn't you?"

"So many questions," the man replied, taking his staff from his back and preparing to use it as a walking stick. "Why should it matter where I came from, anyway?"

"Well, if you really came from the Waste, my family wouldn't laugh at me! They think I've been imagining things."

"Hmm, I could see how that might be important to you, then." He glanced back down the trail. "Is that why you were up there?"

Casber nodded, "Yesterday I saw something, so the Elder ordered me to keep watch and report anything I found. Everyone else thinks I just imagined it! They know nothing about life in the Waste, they think it's just a dead place."

"Well, no desert is ever really lifeless; although, it may look like it... And I'm certain a few might be less than pleased to hear it called a dead place." The man seemed amused. "You should actually just be thankful that I was there to save you from your folly."

Exasperated, he muttered to himself, "And if I hadn't been so busy looking for you I'd never have fallen in the first place!"

The boy followed his rescuer as they continued walking up the path toward Casber's home.

Chapter 5: Unexpected Company

Casber was grinning as he came up the trail with the stranger. His younger cousin, Cort, was the first to see them. He paused to stare back at his cousin in triumph, his companion by his side, then he ran off, shouting, "Papa, Papa!"

That brought uncle Wane and his father, who grabbed their bows as his mother came running, "Casber!"

He stopped and looked down at himself.

"Oh."

He must look quite the sight, he realized, having nearly fallen down the side of the mountain.

"Uh, I'm fine. It was just a little accident."

His mother grabbed him about the shoulders.

"What happened?"

The stranger by his side said helpfully, "The cliff side gave way. I caught him before he could fall far."

"Bal! Someone get Bal with his herbs!"

"Valens, I've got them!" His elfblooded uncle shouted having quickly ducked into his tent to fetch them even as Casber's grandfather, the Elder of Winome Clan, came out of the tent behind him.

He stared at Casber's companion and his walking staff that was almost as tall as the man who bore it.

"Who are you?!" Casber's father, Daffyd, demanded.

"Hmm? I'm George."

"Gee-orj? What kind of name is that?"

Casber's grandfather, the Elder, said, "It's an ogre name."

George looked at him thoughtfully. "An ogre name? How fascinating."

Daffyd glared at him. "You don't look like an ogre."

"That's because I'm not," George replied, glancing at Casber's uncle Balfour who began cleaning the boy's scrapes and scratches.

Casber noticed that Gee-orj seemed particularly interested in his uncle's pointed ears.

"You must be thirsty," his grandfather said. "Someone get our guest some water. I think we would all like to hear your tale."

George leaned on his staff as Casber looked up at him and smiled.

'It could be worse, George,' his DHR model computer whispered in his mind.

"How?" he muttered.

'They could be trying to kill you like so many of the last folk we met.'

Wasn't that the truth? He had made a few friends among them. Then again, plenty of the people, rather large in fact, seemed to think he'd committed blasphemy and wanted to kill him, making his recent leave-taking a bit more rushed. Coming across wyverns hunting him in the Great Waste hadn't made his day yesterday any better.

"Thank you," he said to Casber's mother as she brought him a tin cup filled with clean mountain spring water.

"Thank you for saving my son's life. He's quite the dreamer, which tends to get him in trouble."

George nodded, dreams having become a problem for him as well, lately.

'Perhaps, life is but a dream,' said the staff.

He was careful not to reply to that. Talking to one's self could be considered the mark of a madman, and he had enough problems as it was.

The Elder took his seat across from George and frowned. "Gee-orj, if my grandson is to be believed, you have come from the Great Waste."

"Just passing through."

Daffyd grimaced as Balfour placed a poultice on the deepest gash on his nephew's side.

"No one just passes through the Great Waste. Nothing can live there," replied the Elder.

"I wouldn't tell that to those who do, if I were you. I've found that they take pride in being able to do just that."

38

The Elder said, "You've lived with the trolls?"

George leaned forward. "They call themselves humans."

Daffyd shouted, "Father, this is madness!"

The Elder motioned and Daffyd quieted. "Many call themselves human, but clearly are not…at least not any longer. So, they still live in the Waste," the Elder mused.

"Yes. But I wouldn't suggest trying to pay a visit. They don't seem partial to strangers."

The old man laughed, "No, I don't suppose trolls are. But that begs the question of where you come from. By your outlandish dress, you are not from the Empire. But that cloak of yours makes a statement all its own."

Casber, like many others in the large tent, examined George's cloak, which seemed to be made of a different material than when he had first seen Gee-orj.

Balfour gasped, "You're wearing wyvern hide!"

"Hmm, yes, nice isn't it? Quite warm, actually. It was a gift."

The Elder laughed louder than before, "Quite a gift. First you have to kill the wyvern before it kills you."

Daffyd was even less pleased by the guest than before.

"You shall join us for a meal and we shall continue this conversation," said the Elder.

George was quick to add, "I, uh, don't eat meat."

Casber's father said, "After eating wyvern, I guess, I can understand that."

All laughed.

"Ahem," the Elder uttered and the group fell silent.

"Cheese all right?"

"Yes, just fine."

"Valens, would you be so kind as to see to that?"

After the meal Balfour studied Casber's injuries. Casber had recounted his harrowing escape during the mid-day meal. He realized that the boy had to have taken much more serious hurt, at minimum a bruised rib or broken bone. That he had not suggested something almost impossible.

This Gee-orj might have had the healing gift, but that was certainly not true. He clearly didn't have elvin blood, which was necessary to wield healing mageries. Furthermore, Casber had made no mention of being healed, something the boy couldn't help but notice, since they required such complex spells.

But if Gee-orj had the gift, perhaps he could... No, he thought to himself, *don't even think it. It's hopeless. I don't have the gift.*

Balfour had been tested and tested again. Oh, he learned all the lore, but still couldn't affect a single healing magery.

Still, he watched the stranger, never letting his walking staff stray an inch from his fingertips, wearing the wyvern cloak like a mage out of some fable. He concentrated, focusing on the cloak, poring over its leathery scales. *Who was this man to wear such a thing?*

Casber, meanwhile, was tasked as George's guide. He showed him every aspect of life in the Winome encampment after Balfour released Casber from his examination.

George learned of their wintering in the Fastness, where their herd of sheep were kept safe and fed on the summer stores of grain and grasses.

Balfour glared at his younger brother as he went out to look after the sheep. Casber grinned, no one was laughing at him now.

George assured his young guide, "No one's going to laugh at you ever again, my young friend."

Casber grinned, all the broader.

The Elder peered from behind the woven curtain of the doorway, watching his grandson and Gee-orj.

"Balfour," the Elder called.

"Yes, father?"

"You must tell him."

"What?"

"Something has happened. Don't ask me how, but I know this man from somewhere. Not him, precisely, not his face, but his aura.

There's an enchantment shrouding him. One I haven't felt for many years, except for a passing moment days ago."

"What are you talking about?"

"He's being Summoned, lad," said the Elder.

"But that's madness! Only an adept can—"

"Bal, we've both known adepts."

"Summoned?"

"He'll need a guide and I am far too old for any more adventures."

"Father…"

"You must do this and tell him, tell him all about your failure. Why you are wasting your potential when you should be a real healer!"

Balfour lowered his head. "It's no use."

"And a man who speaks of trolls who still think themselves human, have you ever heard of such a person in any of the tales?"

"Never."

"So dare to believe in yourself, lad. Perhaps he has the answers you need, too."

Casber's cousin, Grace, offered George a cup of watered down wine.

"You must be thirsty, My lord."

"Uh, thank you."

She smiled at him and joined Casber's other teenage girl cousins, who giggled.

George shook his head, "I don't want to know, do I?"

Casber chuckled. "You look a sight better to her than the clansman she'll likely be matched with come winter."

"Matched with? She can't be more than fifteen."

"Fourteen, the same age her sister was when she married in Chasome Clan last winter."

"Hmm," George said, even as a little voice whispered in his mind that Grace's Earthly equivalent age was close enough to fourteen as to make no difference.

41

Balfour came out of the Elder's tent and met his brother and George.

"Gee-orj, I would like to speak with you."

Casber looked up at his uncle when Balfour added, "privately."

"Oh, I'll be off then," Casber said, scurrying off.

George nodded, "What can I do for you?"

"I believe there are truths to be spoken."

George didn't quite like the sound of that.

"Truths I need to share," the half-breed, elfblood, said.

"Oh."

Balfour gestured for him to accompany him and they walked down the path out of the settlement. The elfblood did not speak until they were out of sight of the camp.

"Gee-orj."

"George. It's pronounced, George."

"Jee—orj."

"George."

"Jeeorj."

"Close enough," he said, chuckling.

Balfour relaxed.

"What I am about to tell you is difficult for me to admit. But, I have not always lived with my clan. When I was young, I traveled with my father, Elder Win, after my elvin mother died. Father did not take the loss well. Elves normally live far longer lives than humans. For her to die so young – it was a great tragedy. It was years before Father found love again, and when he did, I was of age to be trained in the healing arts."

He said this as if George should have understood completely. George just patiently listened.

Frowning, Balfour went on, "I went to the Imperial Capital and stayed with my uncle Ofran. I was admitted to the Healer's Hall for training, I learned much, though I couldn't master the magery."

"I don't understand."

"Although I have elvin blood and should be able to wield magery, it is as if I'm human, like my father. You must understand

42

that in the Empire they believe that you must have elvin blood to do magery because elves have souls, unlike humans."

"What?" George muttered with a laugh.

"I know it's a cruel belief. My father has more soul than anyone I've ever met!"

"Bias is a funny thing, isn't it?" George said.

Balfour nodded, "But when someone such as I cannot affect even a simple spell, even given time, well, life becomes unbearable in the Empire. I returned home to Father, my brothers were grown and were marrying by then, starting families.... I am a Clan oddity. But since our mother's death it has been I who has looked after Father."

"Your father loves you very much."

"Yes, which is why he feels I am supposed to guide you to the Empire."

George stiffened.

"Father is certain that is where you are going, Gee-orj. He says you have been enchanted, a Summoning draws you."

George leaned heavily on his staff, "An enchantment, how quaint a description—and damn painful."

Balfour reached out and touched his arm. His fingers tingled at the contact and George recoiled.

'Telepathic dampener's engaging.'

"What?"

"You heard that?" George said.

"Who said that?" Balfour asked.

'Me.' The walking staff glowed ever so faintly to Balfour's elvin second sight.

"What?"

"This is Staff – my often sarcastic companion and left side of my brain these days."

'I am a DHR model computer with full humanistic functionality.'

"Huh?"

George said, "I think we'd both better sit down on those nice logs over there."

Balfour listened, eyes wide as George told the tale of his arrival. "You fell through the Gate?"

"It was definitely a Gateway of some kind, but like nothing my people have ever seen."

Nodding, Balfour said, "It must have been the Highmage's Gate. That you ended up out there in the Waste and not in the Empire is bad. The Highmage would never have intended something like that."

"Really? I suspected that when the dragons fought over whose snack I was going to be."

Balfour leaned back, "But why did the Highmage—and it had to have been the Highmage himself—summon you through the Gate?"

"My question is simpler: how soon can he send me back?"

Balfour shook his head, "The Gate's been sealed for millennia – since the Great War. Gee-orj, I must ask this. I was going to for personal reasons but now I must know for others as well."

He looked deeply into George's eyes as he asked, "Did you heal Casber immediately after his accident?"

George paused a moment, then shrugged and said, "Yes."

"What were his injuries?"

The staff glistened and Balfour mentally heard, 'Broken ankle, two fractured ribs—'

And images, unlike anything he had ever imagined, filled his mind; he saw the damage inside Casber's body.

"And his arm snapped when I grabbed hold," George finished.

"By the Gate, you're a healing mage!"

"What? Oh, definitely not. Staff and I just did some basic first-aid."

"First-aid?"

"Look, I'm an archaeologist. You need lots of skills and training to be out in the field. It can be rather dangerous and those with DHR computers are expected to handle minor emergencies."

"Casber's injuries were truly minor to you?"

"Um, yes."

"Can you teach me these spells?"

"No spells. I don't do magic, my friend. I'm just an archaeologist."

"Archea-gist, this means you are a mage?" Balfour said.

"No, I'm a seeker of things past, I uncover history." Love to uncover history, just didn't imagine walking into some kind of fable.

"Uncovering history and you can heal and fight off wyverns single handedly?"

'He used both hands!' Staff quipped.

George glared at his staff and Balfour burst out laughing.

"There's no spells, just knowing how to use your mind. And you've got the necessary talent. Otherwise, you wouldn't be able to hear Staff."

"So, you can teach me."

"Balfour, I—"

"You need a guide to the Empire. The Summoning is drawing you, and you need someone to be there in case it temporarily cripples you."

"What?!"

"That's what I read in the book about it at the Healer's Hall. It was referred to as a minor side effect."

"Wonderful! Oh, that's just wonderful. Bad dreams and headaches aren't enough, huh?"

Balfour paused, "So on our way, you can teach me this...human mage healing."

"It's not magic."

"You will teach me, then?"

"It's not as simple as that, Balfour," George replied.

'He means that I need to teach you.'

"Staff, stay out of this," George muttered.

'George, we need him. He can teach us about this world and we can teach him. Fair trade.'

Chapter 6: Parting Gifts

"Take me with you, uncle Bal!" Casber pleaded in the Elder's tent.

"I can't, Cas. You're too young and who will take care of your grandfather with me gone? You want me to trust Cort or Niel?"

Casber looked to his grandfather for support. He only smiled, jovially begging, "Please, anything but that, boy!"

"But—but—"

"You can sleep here, lad," his grandfather said. "No more petty torments from your brother or cousins."

Casber's eyes went wide, delighted by this turn of events, as his uncle went to a small intricately carved chest that was part of a set his grandfather said they always had to handle with care. They were elf made and very precious. Balfour opened it and took out a necklace with a lovely polished quartz stone.

The Elder cautiously asked, "Bal, are you sure?"

His uncle Balfour nodded. He offered it to Casber.

"This was my mother's. It is warded against harm. She gave it to me before she died. Wear it always. It will keep you from mage harm, and may even serve as a reminder not to sit on the edge of a cliff."

Balfour dared not look at the old man's face, but Casber saw his grandfather's tears.

"I won't. I promise! I'll wear it always!" Casber assured.

Balfour clasped it about his neck then shooed him out.

Casber cast one last look back as Balfour bade him a tearful farewell.

"You are leaving," Daffyd du Winome said.

"That I am," George answered.

"Good and with my eldest brother, which is better still."

George looked at him. "You hate him?"

"No. I just don't know him. Oh, we all trust him with our lives. His skills will be missed but we've my niece to marry off and there's those who are skilled and single who can join our clan as the bride price."

"Life's that simple?"

"Simple enough, except for Casber. He'll want to go with you."

"He won't be."

"As long as we understand each other."

George nodded as Casber's father, Daffyd, left him, then turned to see Casber, half hidden behind the brush.

"Uh, I didn't mean to eavesdrop. It's just that when I saw you with Papa—" Casber began.

Laughing, George nodded, "Of course not, that would have been rude."

Together, George and Casber walked down the path to the waterfall, a gentle breeze blowing. The clan drew their spring water from this place. Casber sat down on the nearby rocks and watched the water cascade down.

"I, I never said thank you for saving my life."

George smiled, "There's no need, my friend."

"Do you have to go? I mean, you could marry my cousin – we wouldn't lose Uncle Balfour as our healer, then!"

"Uh, I can't." *What an idea*, he thought. "I've got to make my way home."

"Is it far?"

"Very."

The boy nodded. They sat and watched the clear, flowing water. George suffered a moment of dizziness, saw double, gripped his staff tightly, and it flared with light. George shook his head. The Summoning was apparently nudging him to get a move on.

Casber coughed, shaking his head also to clear his dizziness, then rose to follow George, who gave him a quick hug.

"I must be on my way. Your uncle Balfour told me we've daylight enough that if we leave soon we can reach the nearest Way Stop before dark."

Casber nodded, wiping tears from his eyes. "I, I think, I'll just stay here awhile longer."

"Of course. Goodbye, my friend."

The boy nodded and sat back down, muttering, "It's not fair."

'Fair, fair.'

The polished quartz stone glowed beneath his shirt. It was no longer what it had been. It was something more and it was learning.

The clan and their patriarch said their farewells to their guest and Balfour. The elfblood gave quick kisses to his sister-in-laws and nieces, his nephews offered him a firm arm grip, which brought smiles.

Casber watched at a distance, pausing at the edge of the camp to see them off. He closed his eyes. Life would be better than before. No one would laugh at him or call him a dreamer anymore. He would live in his grandfather's tent and watch over him, likely learn more from him than any of the other youngsters in the clan. He smiled. Yes, life would be much better.

He then imagined hearing the sound of hoofbeats and had a dreamy image of a white horse with a glowing horn jutting from its forehead. It came to a halt, turned to gaze at him.

There was a moment of shocked reaction, *'You.'*

He blinked, coming out of his reverie, thinking, *I'd best not mention any odd daydreams to grandfather any time soon. I don't want to spoil it.*

Chapter 7: The Caravan Road

Lord Ryff, a Sire of Cathart, sighed as he drew back the reins. *Too far from home*, he thought, as he looked about.

No member of his house cared to meet his gaze as the entourage of wagons and armed escort came to a halt along the Caravan Road in the southeastern Crescent Lands, which lay between the Empire and the Barrier Mountains.

Circling high above, soared a bird of ill omen. He stared at up at the rare falc, so far from its northern climes. He glanced away before dismounting his horse without comment. His black liveried daughter, Se'and, paused a moment, trying to find something to say, failing, and quickly leading away her father's mount.

Ryff hardly noticed, his thoughts elsewhere.

The fey bird was a grim harbinger, difficult to ignore. It had been following them for weeks, ever since they had left the Empire and begun traveling back down the Caravan Road. The way was long and arduous, but contemplating the alternative of taking ship once more threatened a worse fate. He heard the sound of coughing from the nearest wagon and winced. His son lay near death.

He had taken the boy to the Empire in hopes that their renowned healers could somehow miraculously cure him. But no sooner had they arrived then they were told otherwise.

"M'lord," murmured his older half sister, De'ohr, the Household's Mother Shaman.

Turning, he pondered, "Do you think that falc is somehow attracted to our parade of five score sisters or do you think it truly just follows in the wake of Vyss's impending death?"

Swallowing hard, the shaman replied, "I would prefer to think it seeks to honor us."

He glanced away. "Is it time?"

"Soon, M'lord. In any case, we should proceed no farther."

With a nod, Ryff marched toward his son's wagon. He would spend what time he could with the boy.

Se'and chose to lead the patrol rather than linger. It was too painful to wait, accomplishing nothing more. No one questioned her choice as she fought back tears, leaving the care of her lord sire's mount to a younger sister. She quickly mounted and took command of the group of sisters heading out on patrol.

Urging the horse to a canter, Se'and sought to forget the pall that hovered over each of the sisters. Best do what needed doing, the last thing they needed now was to be raided in these uncivilized lands.

The seven sisters followed close behind the only full-blood sister to Vyss Secondson, who had been hailed as a child of prophecy, the one who would break the Curse that prevented the few men of Cathart from normally siring more than a single son in a generation, or occasionally killed such sons before they could ever father a single child. It was a prophecy that would likely go unfulfilled for yet another ten generations at the very least. But by then her people would likely have perished.

The patrol headed eastward through the rolling hills, which led to the mountain range that they had run parallel to for days now – the range that bordered the Great Waste.

George and Balfour's mountain-bred horses plodded down the trail. George grimaced with each stride and finally brought his mount to a halt.

His elfblooded companion glanced back and chuckled, "Don't tell me you need another break already?"

George glared as he dismounted rather gingerly.

"Balfour, please, don't start. I've told you I'm not used to riding; at least, not riding anything that travels on four legs, anyway."

The Barrier Mountains that were the elfblood's home towered in the distance behind them as Balfour nodded, "At least you don't fall off anymore."

"Should I feel honored by the fact, my dear student? It isn't as if that didn't give you a chance to heal my bruises. Or are you just upset that I'm not giving you a chance to practice mending my broken bones?"

"That injured stray sheep was good enough for that purpose," Balfour replied with a grin as he dismounted and walked beside his dun colored mount, "Gee-orj, my only question is who's teaching whom?"

George took his staff from his saddle strap, reins in his other hand, and led his mount down the trail. The staff sparkled as George walked, bespeaking them both.

'Isn't it enough that I have to share your pain?! George, this – thing you call being "saddle sore" is no more a pleasure for me than you. At least let me desensitize you to—'

"What? Don't tell me you've suddenly realized that being alive is not all it's cracked up to be."

There was a moment of utter mental silence then the staff glistened ever so faintly.

'I am beginning to think I would have been better off enrapport with anyone else's mind but yours, George.'

Balfour fought to hide his grin at the look on his companion's face. Privately, the elfblood found himself continually astonished by both the man and his enchanted staff, or, as he reminded himself, the "damned computer" as Gee-orj referred to it.

"I am not going to get into an argument with a machine with delusions of grandeur, I just won't."

Staff offered instead, 'Balfour, let us at least be productive and continue today's lessons.'

"Please!" Balfour gushed.

George paid little attention to the enrapport lectures and Balfour's verbal replies about what he already knew from his years of training at the Imperial Healers Hall. Those years of frustration had led to him leaving the Hall and the Empire. Balfour du Winome, an elfblood and son of the all too human Elder of the Clan Winome, was unable to perform the slightest mageries necessary to practice the healing arts the Empire was so renowned for.

It was difficult for George Bradley, "Gee-orj" as Balfour and his kin came to pronounce it, to imagine that the people of this world commonly depended on magic to heal wounds and worse. This entire world was so vastly, shockingly, different than Earth. George was an archaeologist with Terran University who found himself falling across the universe to wherever the hell this was: a world settled by a crashed colony ship, a world inhabited by Elves who apparently had changed the laws of science enough that mankind had gone through a great many changes and been left, by appearances, a primitive people. He was lucky to have made a friend in Balfour as he followed the pull of the enchantment that called him ever northwestward toward the Empire.

George had been shocked to recognize the very human talents for healing Balfour displayed, but never was able to utilize. After all, Balfour had always taken for granted that it must be a person of elvin blood who could utter a spell to effect the healing magicks. Balfour and expressed his knowledge that it was impossible for humans to ever "do magic."

Meeting George had challenged those preconceptions, although, on one point George was adamant: "I don't do magic!" Human talents were based in "science," a word Balfour was gaining a healthy respect for, but one that also carried a connotation across the Crescent Lands and the Empire that equaled pity in its reference to the old legends of the human religion that had failed its people so long ago.

George Bradley's study of the past had not prepared him to confront the twisted reality in which he found himself. He had learned about ancient civilizations through what they left behind, the objects and remnants of structures, bits of stone, shards of glass or pottery, their use of plastics, or combustion engines, any number of a thousand other things that, for an archaeologist of his caliber enrapport with a computer, could explore to create a vivid picture of the life in Earth's past.

Still, none of his skills or experience could have prepared him finding himself living so primitively in a world where the laws of physics governed the laws of the universe. Instead, magic ruled this land and his DHR model computer staff was behaving oddly to say the least, and its technical and natural abilities were somehow magnified to an unheard of level by this magic.

He had gone from a dig in northern Europe to this world; one where humanity, with some degree of technology, had fought a terrible war ages past against elves and their magicks, and had nearly been annihilated. The Great Waste lay on the opposite side of the mountain range behind them, a vast desert that George had come to know all too well.

'Let us review surgical technique,' Staff continued. Images flashed through George's mind.

Balfour's expression was almost radiant as he absorbed the lesson like so many others. Day or night, awake or asleep, he learned from the now living machine that was an extension of George's mind. The computer's designers, had they seen it, would never have believed it possible. George almost wished Staff wasn't conscious, then winced as he considered remounting and riding down the trail.

As George was dreading the prospect of remounting his horse his staff suddenly flared and he cried out.

The by-now-all-too-familiar agony gripped him: the Summoning became his world. His mental barriers were struck aside. He heard Balfour's shout of alarm distantly as he fought the enchantment's affects.

'Warning! Rapport levels unstable! George, I am trying to block the magnitude of the Summoning, but I need your conscious help! George, help me! Trying emergency shutdown of humanistic systems!'

George groaned and clutched his chest as the computer shut down his heart. His horse leapt brush as it raced off the trail southeastward, pell-mell. The enchantment that gripped him dropped away. Apparently George's imminent death was far from the spell's desired outcome.

George nearly fell from the saddle as his blazing staff announced, 'Reinitializing sinus rhythm. Sorry about that, George, but it was the only thing left to try.'

He grunted, holding the saddle horn and reins for dear life. Hoofbeats pounded behind him as his elfblooded companion raced to catch up.

"Gee-orj! You all right?"

He struggled for breath then finally muttered, "Stopping my heart, uh, seemed a bit excessive."

'The spell was overriding your body...and our horses too! I'll do it again if I have to!'

In the back of George's mind he could feel the Summoning quail, recognizing a boundary too dangerous to try crossing ever again.

Chapter 8: Harbinger

The falc was old; many of its feathers had long ago gone to steely gray. Its wingspan was greater than the length of the tallest man's body, and at the moment it was utilizing every inch to reach the two riders on the Caravan Road, linking the Empire to the southern city-states and through the Badlands to the distant Cathart. The winds that held the falc aloft whispered to the ancient bird, *Seek their aid for the prophesied one. All is not yet lost.*

So the enemy of the Demonlord followed the urging of the winds, and in turn was noticed by the eight black liveried riders, whose swords and knives glinted with the rays of the late afternoon sun.

Below, Cle'or's keen eyesight noticed the object of the falc's apparent intent first.

"There!" she shouted as the falc dived toward a rider bursting over the brush that hedged the top of the far hill, a rider who suddenly drew to a halt as his companion followed.

Se'and did not know what the falc heralded, but had little doubt as she ordered her patrol to fan out and cut off the pair who might have posed a danger to her impromptu encampment.

Urging her horse to a canter, she blocked their path and drew her sword. She looked into the eyes of the man in a leather cloak, hardly registering the wooden staff in his hand. The next thing she knew there was a tremendous flash of light. Her horse reared, flinging her off her saddle.

The strangers dismounted and rushed to her side. The companion, an elfblood, looked at her and she felt a feather light touch. He took a deep breath and said, "Nothing's broken."

"You're a healer," Se'and rasped.

"Of sorts," he said, glancing at his human companion.

"My brother's dying, please come!"

The falc began circling and let out a caw.

"It looks like you've got a patient, Bal," George said.

Cle'or and the others closed in around them.

"I'm fine!" Se'and shouted, "They're healers!"

55

"I'm not a healer," George replied. "And sorry for what happened to you. I've an aversion to people pointing swords at me."

Cle'or whispered, "Se'and, what happened?"

"I'm not sure but I'll trust that," she said, pointing to the falc winging back toward their camp.

Balfour, meanwhile, thought hard at George and the staff, 'They've got to be Cathartans, but I've never heard of them leaving Cathart.'

Staff commented, 'They look rather competent with all those weapons. The array of daggers is rather amazing.'

Cle'or glanced back at the two riders as the horses cantered back the way the patrol had come. She briefly glared at Balfour, dressed in animal skins, of all things, yet she sensed his appraisal and felt oddly pleased. In the palm of her left hand, she slipped the hiltless throwing dagger back into its sheath.

As they rode Se'and inspected the man with the staff.

"Who are you?"

"I'm George Bradley."

"Jee-orj Bradlei, Je'orj?" she said, struggling to pronounce it. She glanced at the staff bound to the rigging of the saddle, which he could easily grab at need, his odd clothing, then carefully examined his features.

"Are you an elfblood?" she asked.

"Uh, no. Although, my friend is on his mother's side," the blonde haired woman continued to stare at him disconcerted.

"Can you tell us how your brother was hurt?" George asked.

"He's dying, not hurt."

"He's sick?"

The elfblood glanced at his friend riding beside him, who was cringing a bit as he rode.

'Gee-orj,' the tentative thought reached him from Balfour, 'I don't know what I can do about sickness.'

'Leave the diagnosis to me,' the staff said, 'I've an impressive medical encyclopedic database.'

56

George muttered, "Famous last words."

'I'm mortified.'

"You bucket of crystalline chips, don't get cocky when a life's on the line," George muttered.

'Well, we'll see who's more useful, won't we, mister professor of archaeology.'

George's eyes met with Balfour's as they came into sight of the Cathartan camp.

Who are they? George thought.

Balfour heard it clearly through the computer's telepathic link. He focused his thoughts and answered, 'According to the stories, Gee-orj, Carthart is a land southeast of the Great Waste. It's supposedly a beautiful land with only one thing wrong with it. It's cursed. Apparently, only a few men are born each generation. The women outnumber the men thousands to one. The women are reputed to be among the finest warriors and craftspeople in the world, and they take the matter of protecting the few men in their society rather seriously. It's been centuries since the last Cathartan ventured from their lands. I wonder what brought them here of all places?'

"Interesting," George muttered, thinking that the Summoning had been leading them here.

Se'and saw the staff bound beside George's knee glistened ever so faintly. Her ears raised and she shouted to her sisters, "He is a mage!"

Balfour quickly replied, "Ladies, that doesn't quite describe him. He's pure human without a trace of elvin blood."

The falc settled upon the brightly painted peaked roof of the largest wagon, a wooden affair, which had wheels thicker than the others. It ruffled its wings and abruptly squawked as George, Balfour, and the returning patrol halted before it. It abruptly squawked again.

All turned and stared at the bird, as a robed man and dark robed older women stepped from the back of the wagon and stared at the falc as it suddenly leapt back into the sky.

De'ohr stared at the great bird as it winged away, the sense of what it implored echoing through her body before she turned to gaze at the two strangers now in the camp. Her heart pounded. This was the sign, one no one could deny.

"Sire!" she called. "This is the moment my visions have been leading us to!"

Gazing bright with hope, Ryff muttered, "I pray it to be true..." He pleaded to the approaching strangers, "Whoever you are, please, help my son!"

The oddly dressed elfblood and the man with the walking staff hurriedly dismounted and were ushered inside the wagon.

They found themselves being watched across the encampment with suspicion, and another darker emotion by what the computer staff noted as eighty-two black livered women, armed with bows, swords, and a vast assortment of daggers.

"Do you feel it?" George whispered to his companion.

Balfour winced, "I've never felt such pain."

Cle'or headed the curious off and shouted, "They're healers! The falc led us right to them."

Se'and bounded up the wagon steps right behind them.

Through the curtain door the Mother Shaman said, "My lord, please come away."

"I shall not," Sire Ryff muttered, taking hold of his unconscious son's fevered hand.

With a sigh, De'ohr turned and noted Se'and gesturing to her as the two strangers moved to Vyss's pallet. The walking staff flared in the man's hands. "Full body scan," she heard the mutter as the young woman, Fri'il, continued to towel cold water on the boy's fevered brow.

The older woman, Me'oh, who Ryff had taken into his household for her renowned herbal healing skills, looked incredulously at George and Balfour as she heard De'ohr say to Se'and, "The man's a mage?"

The sandy haired Se'and nodded, "They say not, but—"

Vyss's body arched in agony.

58

"What the hell?!" George shouted.

Balfour gasped, "There's no record of such a thing in the Imperial Healer's Archive, Gee-orj!"

"We took him to the Imperial Capital to the Healer's Hall," Lord Ryff said, "They said they could do nothing to save him from the Curse."

"But why couldn't they recognize this for what it is, Gee-orj?" Balfour wondered.

"Would you have?" George rebutted, leaning heavily on his staff. "Let me think. I was half hoping we were dealing with something easy to deal with, like cancer."

Sire Ryff looked about him, "Can you do nothing?"

"Give me a moment, please. My friend and I need to, uh, consult." The staff began to glisten and the two strangers grew still.

Fri'il said, "Who are they?"

Se'and said, "He's Balfour. That's Je'orj. The falc led us right to them, then made it clear that we were to bring them here."

Me'oh gave a concerned look to De'ohr. The Mother Shaman understood. The boy had little time. Whatever they were going to do they had best do it quickly.

Gee-orj, staff hasn't covered this in my lessons, Balfour thought.

George inquired in silence, Staff, what with five thousand years of medical knowledge at your fingertips, there's nothing that covers this one?

'George, I'm cross referencing exorcisms now.'

The archaeologist mentally laughed. *Well, we're here, the boy's dying as we dither. So, I guess it's up to me.*

'George...'

"End conference," the man muttered, "maintain level one rapport."

'Acknowledged. I hope you know what you're doing.'

"I hope so, too," he mumbled as his gaze came back into focus. The young woman bathing the boy's fevered brow couldn't be more than sixteen-years-old on earth. She looked up at him with pleading eyes.

"You'll need to give us some room," George said.

"I'm not leaving," the boy's father said.

"What I'm about to do may disturb you. I really suggest—"

"We're all staying. Fri'il, over there, is Vyss's wife. We're his family," the woman with gray streaked hair said.

"I know my son is dying," Ryff added, "and that he has little time."

George gripped Balfour's shoulder and said, "We need to get those clothes off him. I've got some old fashioned surgery to do."

Me'oh and the young woman Fri'il frowned as they removed Vyss's sweat drenched clothing.

Sire Ryff, the Mother Shaman, and Se'and however only stared at the blade the man drew from its waist sheath. The blade was almost gray, discolored like none of them had ever seen before. The man brought it close to his staff, took a deep breath and closed his eyes. The staff glowed brighter and brighter as did the blade of discolored, now nearly black, metal.

From Balfour's memory everything he knew of the Cathartan's Curse flowed through George's mind. The Curse's onset in its virulent form occurred at puberty. Muscle weakness was the first indication of the disease, which progressed in stages that resembled a wasting sickness. It was presumed that the lads died of the fevers that burn out their human bodies. Little else was known, save that there was no cure.

Me'oh looked up at Balfour, "Vyss is our lord sire's secondson, something more rare than, I dare say, you could understand not being from my land. We sought out the Healers in the Empire with hopes in their magery. But they told us the Curse was far beyond even their knowledge and sorceries."

Balfour frowned, "If anyone can cure him, Gee-orj, can."

"Bal," George muttered, "deep probe him, please. Then monitor and keep your barriers up, just in case."

George then moved to stand over the boy and held his oddly colored dark blade over the boy's body, then muttered, "Activate emergency sterile field."

The staff he held in his left hand blazed with blue light. Me'oh and Fri'il felt a tingling sensation, not unpleasant, just something foreign to their experience. The Mother Shaman's eyes widened as she stared. Her brother, Sire Ryff, gasped, "He's uttered no spell."

His sandy haired daughter said, "Je'orj claims he has no elvin blood."

"And he can wield such magery?" her father asked.

De'ohr stiffened, feeling her visions take her, feeling them whisper to her that this was why her dreams had led them across the world to try to save the boy. Failure to cure him in the Empire was fated. It was this moment upon which the future of their House, the future of her people, rested.

George muttered, "Getting anything?"

'Nothing,' came Balfour's mental reply. *'His heart rate is steadily weakening. It's sucking the life out of him.'*

With an unconscious nod, George passed the blade over the boy's stomach. Still nothing. He moved the blade slowly toward the boy's feet.

Shock. The staff flared, throwing up mental barriers to shield George as the boy cried out. Balfour paled, reeling backward with an image locked before his mind's eye.

A moment later, it was as if nothing happened.

"My, my, wasn't that something? You all right, Bal?" George asked.

The elfblood healer shook himself, "I believe you've found it. Now what?"

George said, "Ladies, please hold him down. It's important he moves as little as possible."

Me'oh and Fri'il frowned as Balfour whispered, eyes wide, "Gee-orj...."

George took a deep breath, thinking archaeology wasn't supposed to be like this, then muttered, "Now for the hard part, I cut it out."

"Did he say cut it out?" Ryff worriedly asked. "Cut what out?"

Bal said, "I think you'd better hurry, Gee-orj."

"Uh, right. Here goes."

"What's he doing?!" the boy's father bellowed as Me'oh and Fri'il gasped.

George brought down the blade and—

BOOM!

It wailed. The wagon quaked, knocking everyone standing off their feet except George, who seemed rooted. Vyss woke screaming an eerie, unearthly howl as Me'oh and Fri'il fought to hold him down.

The dark blade drew blood as George's staff flared to incandescence. BOOM! again.

The wagon wheels collapsed and a foul smelling smoke made them all cough as it poured off the boy's body.

The next thing George knew he heard the boy's father shouting, "Vyss! What's happened to Vyss!"

Hands were pulling back the canvas roofing as George and Balfour coughed.

Me'oh muttered, "By all the Lords of Cathart, what has happened?!"

George gasped, using his staff to help him push aside the blankets, assorted vials of herbal remedies, and the teapot that had fallen across him. "One demon excised," he groaned. "I hope."

The teenage girl was waving smoke away from her face when Vyss coughed, "Fri'il?"

She stared at him, "M'lord?"

"Fri'il, I'm cold." The boy tried to sit up. "Hey, I'm not wearing any clothes!"

There was a sudden silence.

"Vyss?"

"Poppa?"

"Vyss! See to him, I'm fine! Hear that, De'ohr, my boy's alive!"

"Well, Gee-orj, at least they don't want to kill us."

"That's most definitely an improvement," George said with a chuckle as he washed his face in a cold water basin the ladies had provided.

#

They had been given a rather fine looking tent as the Cathartans readied a celebratory feast in their and young Lord Vyss's honor.

"M'lords," Fri'il said from the doorway. "If you would, we would wash your garments."

"You think you can wash the demon stink off them?" George asked.

She smiled, "It seems to come out with soap rather nicely. In the meantime, I've brought you some of Sire Ryff's extra robes."

They were beautiful, George thought, a cross between an ancient Japanese kimono and a silk garment similar to a skirt, though styled for men.

"Thank you," Balfour said.

"Just set your clothes to be cleaned out here and I'll be back for them."

They nodded as she left, the George said, "Well, Bal, feel like a surgeon yet?"

His elfblooded companion laughed, "Not your normal surgery."

"No," the archaeologist replied, wondering just what he'd gotten himself into.

"You can't be serious, Father!" Se'and shouted.

"They saved your brother's life. I can do no less!"

The Mother Shaman intervened, "You must do more, Sire."

"What?" Lord Ryff said, frowning.

"They've made the Prophecy possible again! You must do more than make them Cathartan Lords."

Se'and reiterated, "You can't!"

Her father sat back, "Se'and, De'ohr's right. This is a matter of honor. I'm sorry, but there is no other way."

"I'm not marrying him!"

Dinner was a truly magnificent affair. Young women performed songs, dances, and acrobatics. Cle'or was featured with the dance of knives, tossing daggers in the air like a juggler, while executing precise katas, as those in the eastern part of earth. She bowed as Sire Ryff slapped George's back.

"She is my House's finest champion!"

"Wonderful," he said.

Sire Ryff glanced at his older half sister and nodded. She made a mental note.

Se'and personally served George a choice piece of the game they'd recently taken. She wasn't smiling, which earned her a glare from her father. So she bowed rather invitingly to George, who found himself hastily needing to look up into the young woman's eyes.

"Uh, thank you, but I don't eat meat."

She frowned, "Do you prefer fish or cheese?"

"Cheese is fine, but I don't eat fish either."

She bowed again, giving him the requisite view as honor demanded then left to fetch him a serving of cheeses.

Me'oh saw her stalking past.

"Se'and," she said gently, "it might not be that bad."

"He refused my offering! Who does he think he is?"

"Oh," was all she said with an amused look as the young woman headed back to the kitchen, then, "Oh, you have it bad, don't you."

Balfour was drinking the Imperial wine. Tasting it, he knew it an excellent vintage. He remembered sharing a bottle with—well best not dwell on that. *She is likely married by now and I had been a failure at the Healer's Hall, after all.*

Staff twinkled across the room where George sat as Se'and returned with a heaping platter of cheese.

'Bal, you're not a failure,' Staff mentally said to him. *'Stop thinking that way. Your talent is just on the human side of the equation.'*

Through the link he heard George say, "Thank you," to the young woman, who was wearing a rather tight fitting and revealing dress.

"May I join you?" he half heard Se'and ask George.

"Uh, sure," George replied scooting over on the pillow that served as his chair.

'Bal, is there something about Cathartan morés I should warn George about?'

'I don't think so,' he replied, watching George's reactions to his environment.

The herbalist, Me'oh, brought Balfour a plate, "I brought you some fruit."

"Thanks. Uh, bringing fruit doesn't have any special meaning, does it?"

Me'oh chuckled, "Not fruit, no."

He watched her walk away and thought at the staff, *'Uh, you might want to mention to George—'*

'Oh, don't give it another thought,' Staff replied. If Balfour didn't know better by now, he would have thought that the computer was laughing.

Se'and edged closer to George, "You were heading west when we found you."

"Uh, yes, Bal and I are going to the Empire."

"You do not speak with an Imperial accent. Where are you from?" she asked.

"Oh, from quite a distance, you wouldn't have heard of it."

"I have studied the geography of the entire known world. Being Vyss's only full blooded sister, I was expected to manage the affairs of his House."

"Well, I'm from someplace I doubt you'd have heard of," George replied.

"Pray tell!"

"Well, I most recently lived in Europe, for example."

"Urp?"

"Yes, quite a historic place really. Gave me plenty to do."

"Do? You are a mage, yes? Or a healer?"

He laughed. "No, I'm an archaeologist, a department head at the University."

"Arki-mage at uni–ver–sity?"

65

"Close enough."

She frowned, "You really have no elvin blood?"

"No, and of that I can guarantee, I have the DNA scans to prove it."

"You are a very strange man," Se'and said.

"Believe me, since coming to these parts I've seen stranger."

She glanced at her father, who was smiling and nodding to her as her brother, Vyss, watched closely, and realized what their father intended. Vyss hurriedly rose and took Fri'il's hand; she had been sharing his seat cushion and had served him at the beginning of the meal.

Se'and got the oddest feeling that the staff was somehow focusing on her, staring at her curiously. It also twinkled, as if winking at her.

George glanced at the staff, paled a bit, then took a rather large gulp of wine before hastily rising.

"Uh, you'll have to excuse us."

"Us?" she muttered as he marched off with his mage staff.

George had no sooner gone out of the tent than Vyss and Fri'il followed. Outside Vyss overheard Je'orj muttering, "You could have warned me!"

Fri'il and Vyss exchanged glances as George, seemingly chastising himself, paused. Fri'il looked at Vyss pensively.

"Are you all right, Vyss?" Fri'il asked, worried.

"I'm fine. Father's got to be planning to bond Se'and to him," he said, ignoring Fri'il's concerns for his health.

"What?"

"It makes sense, he saved my life."

"Yes, but making Je'orj an honorary Lord of Cathart is likely something out of the old stories about Lord Kyrr."

The conversation paused as Vyss looked upon his wife with the same look of concern she had given to him.

"Fri'il, I know you and I haven't—"

"Vyss, I was given to you as your wife. I knew you were sick and what was expected of me. If it were at all possible, I know we—"

"And, uh, it wasn't, was it?"

"No, it wasn't. But it is now, isn't it? Do you want to, um…"

"No! That wasn't what I brought you out here to discuss. Fri'il, it was my life Je'orj saved. I have so little to show the honor I owe him."

Her eyes widened. "You don't mean… oh."

The moment was punctured by Sire Ryff shouting back at the celebration.

"Cle'or, where has our guest of honor gone?"

She gestured to a half dozen others and they hastened out. "Se'and, did you say anything to offend him?"

"Nothing, M'lord!"

"Hmm, De'ohr!"

Balfour moved to slip out but a couple of black liveried women cut him off, "Please sit, M'lord. Sire Ryff wishes to express his thanks to you and your companion."

Me'oh came back with dessert as the elfblood hesitated. She asked, "Would you join me at the table?"

"If you promise to tell me what's going on," he replied.

"It'll only be a guess."

"Lead on, then."

De'ohr frowned at their sitting down together.

Outside, George was having his own meeting. "Of all the–! What are your crystalline circuits using for brains, Staff?!"

'Now, George, when in Rome…'

"Don't give me that. Yes, she's damn attractive, but if they think I'm going to sleep with her as—"

"Ahem, M'lord Je'orj?" a feminine voice inquired.

He turned around and saw Cle'or with a dozen of her unsmiling friends.

"If you'd be so kind as to return to the dining tent, Sire Ryff would like to express his gratitude more fully."

'George, don't make a scene. They seem more annoyed than seriously threatening.'

He half whispered, "I noticed that."

George smiled and nodded at the women, gesturing for them to lead the way, saying, "Of course."

Chapter 9: Gifts

"Ah, our guest of honor has returned at last," Sire Ryff said as he rose from his divan. "All here know of how you have saved my stricken son, Vyss, from death's door. This festival meal is not enough to express our thanks. The Curse has been the bane of our people for thousands of years. Our greatest prophecy says that when a secondson has a secondson, the Curse will be forever broken. My son Vyss is the first secondson born in nearly four centuries. Your healing him, casting the evil that we could not see from him offers us the promise of the Prophecy in our generation!"

There were cheers and applause all around.

"I couldn't have done it without Balfour here."

"Oh, yes, you could have!" the elfblood quickly shouted back, glancing in shock at the herbalist, Me'oh, beside him, who had given him a very clear idea of what gift Sire Ryff was about to bestow. "Really, it was all his doing!"

George motioned to Balfour, "You're too modest, my friend!"

"Not this time," he muttered, "oh, well, no good deed goes unpunished, my father always says." Balfour covered his eyes.

The Mother Shaman stiffened, sensing a sudden stillness all about them. She hardly dared to breathe as she felt something focusing intently. First she feared it was centered on her brother or nephew. She realized it was focused on George.

Sire Ryff said, "We must honor you both for your deeds this day. Je'orj du Bradlei, Balfour du Winome, for saving the life of Vyss, the secondson, I pronounce you lords by bond. Rise, my daughter, Se'and, greet thy lord husband, Lord Je'orj.

"Rise, my wife, Me'oh, herbal healer of the People of Cathart. I free you of your charge of my life and that of my now healthy son, and bind you to these men. See to their care, learn from them and teach them, choose between them who shall cleave to them for the remainder of their days. Cle'or, my daughter, champion of this house, I bind you as champion to their houses. Choose between them who you shall cleave to for the remainder of your days, and safeguard them always on their journey."

There was utter silence for a moment.

"Father!" Vyss shouted from the tent's entry, "I, too, would honor them for saving my life. I have but one precious offering: my wife, Fri'il, who has to this day remained only affianced, I bind to the houses by bond of Je'orj and Balfour. Beloved, first of my house; choose between them who you shall cleave to for the remainder of your days, safeguard them on their journey, and bear them strong and healthy daughters!"

His father nodded, "Such is your right. Such is the honor due. None shall contest your choice, nor my will, in this!"

Every woman in the room bowed as George stood dumbfounded, then glanced at Balfour who mentally explained.

"What do you mean, married?!" he shouted.

De'ohr felt a rush of air drive her to the ground. She collapsed and heard an exultant shout as she lost consciousness.

"See to De'ohr! Fetch me the moment she wakes!" Lord Ryff ordered.

"Uh, Sire Ryff," George said, "excuse me, but you really don't—"

"I understand, it is no easy responsibility I give to you both, but women are very good at dealing with obstacles. Cle'or can see to their ongoing weapons training, particularly the young woman, Fri'il's. She comes from a long line of respected sword swains. My lovely daughter, Se'and, is strong and will bear you many healthy daughters. And, with Me'oh, her herbal knowledge should aid your own healing efforts nicely, Master Balfour."

"But, Sire Ryff, you don't understand," George protested, trying not to look at the four rather attractive women. "I'm, uh, not from around here."

"He's going to the Empire, Father," Se'and said, feeling torn.

"Then this gift is a double boon to you," Lord Ryff stated. "They can protect you."

"I really can protect myself," George said.

"Even a mage needs mortals to watch over them," Ryff said.

Se'and glanced at her husband's backside. "Hmm."

George caught that look and seemed at a sudden loss for words. The staff twinkled.

Once back in their tent, George said, "Let's make a break for it."

"Gee-orj, I don't think that's really a goo—"

Balfour was interrupted by Se'and entering and carrying her livery in a bundle, along with her sheathed sword.

"My lord, where are you planning to sleep?"

He stared at her, searching for the right words. "Ah, I don't think I'm going to sleep tonight."

She gave him an unreadable look, "If that is your wish."

"Uh, no, I didn't mean it that way," he said, blushing.

She smiled, "I'd hoped not, M'lord, but, I'm… willing."

Balfour coughed awkwardly as Me'oh came in with her bundle and sword. "Where you sleeping, M'lord?"

He choked.

Se'and neared George and said, "I know this is awkward, but can you help me unbutton my dress."

"Um."

"I'll help with that," Me'oh said.

George turned his back and realized he was facing a mirror. He turned to the left, facing another mirror as Se'and's dress fell to the floor. She smiled at him in the mirror, noticing his staff was doing that strange twinkling thing again.

Outside, the Mother Shaman stood beneath the stars, speaking to the sky.

"I know you are there."

Hmm, can't fool you.

"What are you doing here?"

I mean no harm to you or yours.

"Who are you?"

An interested party, nothing more.

"I don't believe you."

Vyss, the secondson lives, isn't that enough?

"Why are you watching Lord Je'orj?"

As he has helped your people this day, I believe he can help the world.

"I sense much more."

You are wise. Know this: your House's fate lies with his.

"That was fated from the moment he saved Vyss's life."

Likely longer than that. Hence a boon I would ask in both our interests.

"I make no promises to unseen creatures."

Merely consider is all I ask. Je-orj seeks to leave our lands forever. Warn your bound kinswomen that he must not. They must do all in their power to bind him to our fates. Else, I fear, the world shall have no hope.

"You ask them to only do their duty to their newborn House."

No, I ask they do much more than their duty – else all may be lost.

"Bal, you're not making this any easier," George said to his smirking friend.

"So. I'm watching, so what? You want to take down those heavy mirrors?"

"Great idea. Come help!"

"I can help with that," Me'oh said.

"No, just get dressed for bed, we can handle this," George said.

"We are dressed, as you call it, for bed," Me'oh said.

"Shit," George muttered.

"Is something wrong?" Se'and asked, standing with her hands on her hips. "If the mirrors really bother you we're more than happy to help move them, M'lord."

"Just cover them up... Please," George rasped, shutting his eyes, face flushed.

George and Balfour slept back to back that night. Me'oh frowned and Se'and shrugged. It made for a peculiar wedding night.

Fri'il said hesitantly, "Which one should I, uh..."

Cle'or said, "Does it matter? Try either one out, then the other. That's what they did in the old stories anyway."

72

George rolled over with a groan, feigning sleep. He found himself facing his loudly snoring friend. Staff laughed.

"Stop it!" George mumbled.

There was a rustling.

Se'and peered down at him, "Something wrong?"

He squeezed his eyes tightly shut. "Nothing, bad dream."

She paused then bent and kissed his cheek, "Good night, husband. We'll leave at first light."

"Good." It couldn't come soon enough for him. Se'and left him in peace.

More rustling, a kiss on the cheek, "Good night, M'lord."

More rustling.

'This is going to be a long night, isn't it, George?'

A light whisper, "Good night, M'lord."

Later, more rustling as someone lay down beside George.

"Hey," George said in surprise.

Se'and said, "I'm cold... Just cold."

"Oh."

'Is she cute or what, George?'

Mass rustling. Balfour woke, "Hmm... Mmmm, Cle'or?"

"Just, uh, cold, M'lord."

There was giggling.

It made for a hell of a long night.

Chapter 10: History of a Dagger

George awoke at dawn and slapped away an insect crawling up his leg, still feeling weak and tired due to the Summoning's pressure throughout the previous day.

Wonderful, just wonderful, he thought.

'It could be worse, George,' the all too familiar voice whispered in his mind.

"I know," he mumbled, rubbing sleep from his eyes.

"Morning, M'lord," Cle'or said, having apparently been on guard duty.

He looked at the blonde-haired woman sword swain with the deep scar across her face, a member of his unwanted escort.

'George, I don't think body guard describes her well enough,' the computer staff whispered.

He coughed as his elfblooded friend Balfour and the other three black liveried women of their escort rose from their blankets. The youngest, Fri'il, smiled at him as she paused to lace back up her bodice before donning her plain livery.

Oh, boy, he thought.

She smiled all the more as he looked away, which was when he realized that Se'and, the sandy haired leader of his escort, was watching him.

"Uh, good morning," he said.

"Morning, M'lord."

"I am not really into this 'M'lord' stuff."

"Sorry, M'lord… Would you rather we call you Sire?" Se'and asked.

"Uh, no."

"Husband, then?" she asked with a look of dead seriousness.

"No!" George shouted.

"You are, nonetheless," she replied.

"No, I definitely am not."

"Se'and, don't push him," said the slightly older Me'oh, the trained herbalist. "Having us bonded to him and Balfour here is not something that happens every day."

Balfour approached.

"Gee-orj and I both feel Sire Ryff and Vyss's generosity is a bit…misplaced."

"You saved my brother, Vyss's, life," Se'and said, "my father's gratitude can know no bounds."

"And the two of you need looking after," Cle'or said, dancing a dagger on her fingertip.

"Leaving you two out here alone will likely get you killed… And I, for one, am happy to kill anyone who tries to harm you."

"I, as well!" said Fri'il, who couldn't be more than sixteen years old, in standard earth years.

"Don't get ahead of yourself, lass," Cle'or said. "Practice, practice, practice."

"Yes, Ma'am."

Se'and shook her head, assuring the male travelers, "We're yours, M'lords. Accept it and let us do our jobs. Siring babes can wait."

George shook his head, "More than wait: you see, I've no intention of staying on this world any longer than I have to. I've a life on my own world, and I've no plans to start a family by traditions that are not my own."

'Live a little, George,' Staff whispered.

"Shut up!" he rasped as Balfour coughed hard trying not to laugh as the four women looked at George in puzzlement.

After George's pronouncement breakfast was a quiet affair. Balfour sat next to him and the four Cathartan women across from them.

Fri'il broke the silence by asking, "What did you mean by going back to your own world?"

Balfour grinned, "Jee-orj isn't from around here. He fell through the Gate."

"The Gate? But that's only a legend," Se'and said.

"For a legend it's a hell of a drop," George replied. He took the edge of his cloak in his left hand, "And the wyverns were no fun either."

75

That got all of Cle'or's attention.

"You fought a wyvern?"

"Several. So you see," George said, "I don't need your help."

"It sounds to me just the opposite," Se'and said. "It sounds like you need all the help you can get, Sire."

"Don't call me that!"

"Je'orj then, but that does not negate the fact you need us."

"Fair enough, but that doesn't make us married."

Se'and just smiled back and Fri'il grinned.

Cle'or said, "I think you better tell us this tale, so we know what we're up against and what your plan really is. Because," she said, waving one of her throwing daggers, "I need to know where I need to throw this."

George sighed as Balfour nudged him, "Jee-orj, you can't do this alone. We can't. I can serve as your guide but Cathartans are legendary for their swordsmanship."

Drawing out his own dagger, he held it out. The metal was dark, nearly black.

Se'and was mesmerized at the sight of it. Me'oh had mentioned George using something like it to heal her brother, but until this moment she did not recognize what it was.

She glanced at her half sister Cle'or, who rasped, "That's an alloy like a Black Blade, a work of anti-magery like the black swords of Cathartan legend. Where did you get it?"

"Where? In Prect in the Great Waste. A friend gave it to me." They stared at him, knowing no one and nothing lived in the Waste. "A most unusual friend."

"Tell us," Fri'il begged. "Please, M'lord, I mean, Je'orj." Slowly the other Cathartan escorts began adopting Balfour's pronunciation of his name. It confounded George, since no one in this world could speak his name as he did, himself.

He sighed and continued, "I awoke somewhere unexpected...."

Chapter 11: Dining with Trolls

"Wot ure oo dinkin' bringin' 'im 'ere?" a man half shouted as he awoke.

"Oo wantet mi ta leaf 'im?"

"Luk at 'im! Ee's so oogly!"

George's fingertips touched his DHR computer that lay beside him on the wide cot. He squinted as the computer staff flared brighter than he could ever remember. It lit the room and gave him, and his hosts, a much better view of each other. He mentally reached out to those about him and the translation program locked into place, adjusting to the dialect changes.

"Such light! It hurts my eyes!"

"Engage dampeners," George muttered.

The computer crystal's light dimmed, yet was still brighter than George was used to.

"Well, if we had any doubts about Greth's story, this should settle them," the woman, Mendra, said.

"That staff is, indeed, powerful. Oh, and you're right, Berrick. He really is quite ugly."

"Mendra!"

He was still in the damned nightmare. *Great. Just great, a nightmare with giants with faces no one would ever want a small child to see, not if you wanted them to ever be able to go to sleep again.*

'George, I'm picking up a signal.'

"Keep on that," he muttered as he sat up with a splitting headache. "Ow," he muttered, bringing his hands to his aching head.

"He's so short, Qapin," Mendra commented.

"That's because Greth's brought home a human."

"No, we're human, what he is, is plain ugly," Berrick said.

"Councilman Berrick! That's enough," Qapin bellowed.

The very tall woman leaned closer, "What you eat, little manling?"

'Now ain't that the question?' the staff whispered in his counterpart's mind.

77

George coughed, realizing there appeared to be something wrong with the DHR computer. He inspected it closely.

The large trolls that surrounded George craned their necks, wondering why he was so rapt with his staff.

"Oh, sorry, I'm just getting used to a new relationship with my computer." His hosts stared at him, looking confused. "Nevermind. I'm George. Where the hell am I?"

'George.'

He ignored the mental voice.

"Welcome to Prect," said the deadly looking troll, whose face looked vaguely familiar. He blinked, realizing that face was the last thing he saw before losing consciousness after he fell through the hole in the universe.

"I am Greth. My scavenger party found you at Ashra Kodiu, the old Elvin city."

"Elvin city?"

"This is my father, Qapin, leader of all Prect. This is my Aunt Mendra, who leads the hospital wardens, and this is Berrick, Chief Councilor of Prect."

'George, I've got something. It appears to be a ship's Mayday. The signal's very faint, very low power. It is identifying a damaged colony vessel in need of assistance.'

George coughed and quietly commanded, "Scan."

'Commencing scan.' Images filled George's mind, images of deck upon deck, combined cabins and other chambers. Each modified to accommodate the height of those who dwelled here. This once had been a colony starship, one that had taken damage beyond the ravages of time.

"He appears to be much frailer than we humans," Mendra said as she knelt beside George and placed a patch on his forehead. It immediately changed color. "If he were human, at this temperature, I would say he is dying."

George shook his head, "No, my body temperature is normal for me, but thank you for your concern."

"You hungry?"

"Uh huh."

Mendra shoved Berrick out of her way, "I'll be back with some tea, biscuits, and neobutrae, which should do nicely."

"Uh, thanks, I think."

"We put neobutrae on all our food. Good protein source," Qapin said as the Councilor glared at George, who smiled back, figuring that was safest.

'George, we're in a downed starship and it's been here a very long time. Longer than when colony ships first began leaving Earth's Solar System some 2,148 years ago. This ship appears to be thousands of years older than that, George.'

Curious, he thought as Greth gave him what he hoped was a reassuring look.

It was hard to tell coming from a ten foot tall leathery skinned nightmare with kind blue eyes.

Fri'il gasped, "The trolls let you live?"

"Let him finish his fanciful tale, young lady. Trolls, indeed!" Se'and said.

Seeing as he had their full attention, George placed his staff across his knees and continued telling it.

The neobutrae was nothing like butter, but Staff did a quick scan that showed it wasn't going to kill him. He guessed the taste was in the eye of the beholder, too. They watched him eat each and every bite.

"Uh, I'd like to go back the way I came."

"Through the Gateway?" Qapin half choked.

"Yes."

"We're not even sure how you managed to make use of it."

"Hmm," he muttered. *Great. Just great.* "In that case, can I get a tour?"

"A tour?"

"Of the *Questor*."

Qapin's eyes went wide. "Where did you hear that name?"

George heard the computer staff say, *'Ah, George, you seemed to have pulled it directly from the neural interface.'*

George hadn't asked for that information. He blinked. That wasn't how a DHR computer with a data/human rapport interface should work. The user asks and it shares. *You didn't just suddenly know.*

George decided truth was always the best policy, especially with hulking trolls. He answered Qapin, "The ship knows its name."

"It's called Prect." Greth said, disapprovingly.

"No, it's the Colonizer *Questor*, Mars Registry 675-B."

"Who told you that?!" Councilor Berrick cried.

"It's in the Mayday. It's still broadcasting."

"What?!" Mendra shouted as part of the troll chorus.

"You don't know the ship's broadcasting?" he asked.

"This is intolerable!" the councilor said.

"Berrick, we'll handle this!"

"No, this is a matter for the Council!"

Qapin grinned, "Really?"

The councilor stared at him. "You wouldn't! I'm Chief Councilor! The Council won't stand for this!"

"Actually, I believe you'll find they understand this falls in my area of responsibility."

Grumbling, Berrick left as Qapin ordered, "Greth, get that fool Lawson!"

And that was how George met the dwarf troll, Lawson. He was only six feet tall and was easy to mistake for one of the troll children running through the corridors that served as streets. He was like the young trolls, closer to human norms. "You called, Qapin?" Lawson said as he arrived.

"Yes, our human friend, George, here tells us that the ship's name is *Questor*."

Lawson stared at me. "Who told you the Holy Name?"

Qapin said, "He told me, and it was the ship that told him. It is board-casting a May-day."

"It's board casting? I've read about that in the Sacred Manuals, but it shouldn't be. The Comm Board is dead, so it can't be board-casting."

"Show me the Comm Board," George said.

"Show him the Board, Greth. Lawson, escort them and keep this quiet. Berrick's already screaming that we should offer his staff to the Power Plant."

"What?!" *What?!* George said, shaking his head at the mental echo.

Greth reassured George, "Don't worry. No one's taking that from you."

Lawson stared at the crystalline staff. "What is that?"

"My computer."

"And it works?"

"Sorta."

'George!' the staff protested.

George was led to the alternate bridge, the backup in case of catastrophic failure of the main system. Staff scanned as Lawson led them through the corridor to the main bridge, which was badly damaged.

The alternate bridge was much better.

Lawson pointed, "The Comm Board's over there."

"Full scan," George muttered, holding the staff directly before him.

It glowed so brightly he winced.

'Commencing. Anomalies noted.' A diagram of the room filled George's mind as he closed his eyes.

He pointed to the right, "The Comm Board's over there, Lawson. That's Auxiliary Control."

Lawson and Greth stood in awe as the Comm Board lit up and a broken monitor activated, "...ayDay, this is *Questor*, Mars Registry 675 Dash B. We have made a forced landing. Off course due to drive failure. Mayday, this is *Questor*, Mars..."

George waved his hand and Staff deactivated the audio. Greth and Lawson were dumbfounded. There was a data stamp in the comm data that had been lost in the transmission. The ship had landed there two thousand years ago, but staff dated the landing here at 5609 years previous, with a standard deviation of ten years maximum. Archaeology was their business. The time discrepancy raised more questions, but facts were facts. George was here in a downed starship that may have passed through a time warp due to their drive failure. If that were the case, only arriving three thousand or so years earlier was a stroke of pure luck.

Looking at his new troll friends, George knew they had paid a terrible price for remaining here. The low levels of radiation weren't lethal in the short term, but the mutation they'd suffered made the long term results to their genetic make-up clear enough.

When George and the trolls returned to the others, Berrick's qualms worsened.

"How could you allow him onto the bridge?"

"Berrick, it was my decision to make!" Qapin yelled back.

"What damage did he do?" the Councilor demanded to know.

"Damage? He fixed the Comm Board and rerouted external sensors to it, which can warn us of encroachments like it was designed to thousands of years ago."

Berrick was livid, "He damaged the Holy of Holies!"

"What?!" George shouted. "It's a miracle the systems work at all."

"It's magery!" Berrick shouted. "We take our power from the enchantments left behind, and our power systems need more power. We need your staff's energy!"

"Berrick!" Qapin shouted as George held his staff tighter, which began to blaze in a reflection of his anger.

Berrick leapt toward him and sought to tear the staff from his grasp. The gray haired troll bounced off the defensive field and hit his head and dropped like a stone. Greth knelt beside the unconscious counselor as George said to Qapin, "No one's messing with my staff."

"I wouldn't have it any other way," Qapin said. "Berrick's a real idiot."

George nodded as Lawson studied the staff from a distance and noted, "That was a shield, like the manuals say the ship had."

"Similar principles," he replied, seeing Lawson getting ready to launch into another discussion about the ship's systems.

"Qapin, can I take him to the Core?"

"Best now while Berrick's unconscious."

"The Core," George said. "You mean the computer core?"

Lawson nodded.

The *Questor's* computer core was a rather dark place to visit. It was like entering a cave.

George held Staff up. It provided better quality illumination than Lawson's torch. "Well, this is it, George."

Greth said, "I'll stay on guard out here. Whatever you do, be quick about it."

"No one but me ever comes here," Lawson said.

"Let's hope it stays that way," Greth said.

George declared, "Scan."

'Commencing scan. Anomalies detected. Functionality is erratic. Core is operating but at an extremely slow speed.'

George dropped into deeper rapport with the staff and could perceive what it meant. A fraction of a data stream appeared in George's mind, an action that should have appeared in closer to a microsecond was slowly registering as time went by.

"It's out of phase."

'Or, looked at another way, it is perhaps we who are out of temporal phase, George.'

"The difference between say a thousand years passing and over five thousand?"

'Hypothetically.'

"George? Can you make it work?" Lawson asked.

"It's already working, just at a pace too slow for you to work with it."

"Perhaps, if you uplink to it," Lawson suggested.

"Uplink?"

"Using the headset, it's too small for anyone else other than the kids and me, or you. It's why Qapin's given me access. He told me to tell no one, but the Core could be of great help to us."

He led George to a recessed command module with a seashell shaped headpiece that was designed for human interface. It had a sim visor, something George had only seen in museums and archival images.

George sat down and put it on. Nothing happened. "Staff, extend rapport, maintaining shields in case of feedback."

'Acknowledged. Extending rapport under shielding. Seeking uplink.'

Outside Greth called out, "I heard something down the hall. I'm going to check it out, be right back."

"Fine, fine," he heard Lawson say as the computer bank in front of him began to glow, matching the warm inviting light staff now cast.

A diagnostic flashed through George's mind.

QUESTOR: IDENTIFY
GEORGE BRADLEY, TERRAN UNIVERSITY.
NOT FOUND
ACADEMIC OVERRIDE, TERRAN UNIVERSITY,
ARCHEOLOGY DEPARTMENT,
RESEARCHER GEORGE BRADLEY, MASTER
COLONIZER FLEET PROTOCOL, CODE A – 50U78093 – ADD
TO QUESTOR'S CREW DIRECTORY.
CREW MAN GEORGE BRADLEY ADDED.
WELCOME ABOARD CHIEF ENGINEER.

George's concentration was broken by Lawson, shouting, "Hey! You can't!"

Then, George was struck from behind. Staff flared as he lost consciousness and he felt the computer staff wrenched out of his hand. He writhed in agony, then knew nothing more.

"It was that Berrick, wasn't it? I'll kill him!" Cle'or shouted.

"They took your mage staff?" Se'and asked.

"Computer staff; I don't do magic. And yes, he did."

'Which is how we learned about our little problem,' Staff commented.

George nodded, "Which is how I learned about another change in my relationship with this fellow, here," he said as he stroked the handle of his staff.

"What change?" Balfour asked, George never having shared this tidbit before.

"Oh, my computer friend and I can't be parted at least by any great distance."

'Five point six feet to be exact.'

"What happens?" Se'and asked.

"We die," George said.

"Ladies, remember," Se'and said, "Staff stays with Lord Je'orj here."

Fri'il swallowed, "So, what happened next?"

George sighed and told them.

Councilor Berrick and his men had an accident when they took staff, one which Greth later explained resulted in quite an explosion. The Core wasn't damaged, however, it just started glowing.

George awoke in agony on that big cot in the guest room of Greth's family residence as Qapin brought Staff back to George.

"What happened?" George groggily asked.

Qapin sat down beside him. "I must ask your forgiveness."

"Just tell me what happened."

Qapin shook his head.

George felt something was different about the staff. It wasn't as cool to the touch. George looked at it and found it covered in some leathery material.

"George, I'm very sorry for what happened. My people were being superstitious fools. Berrick and his friends apparently thought that your staff would power our systems for years to come. But when he took it from you, while you were linked to the Core, he learned the price of his foolishness."

"Qapin, what happened?"

"Berrick lost his hand. I suppose it could have been worse, he could have lost his life. Then the staff just went black. It was dead and Lawson thought you were, too."

George uttered, "Staff, report."

'Systems coming back online. What happened?'

Qapin shamefully looked away and explained, "You reactivated the Core. It is rather displeased with our behavior."

He fixed his eyes on George and explained further. "It refers to you as the ship's Chief Engineer, highest ranking officer presently on board... I suppose that means my title as Qapin passes to you, Sir."

George laid his head back. "Great. Just great."

Dinner was an interesting affair. It was troll formal. Sadly, Councilor Berrick was not able to make it. Mendra broke that news as the guests arrived.

"Chief Engineer," each said, formally acknowledging George as they passed him. George looked up at them and acknowledged, feeling like a child. He shook a lot of hands: city councilors, and that of the Holy Archivist of Prect, who held George in his gaze throughout the evening.

Lawson whispered, "He's Berrick's brother-in-law."

Well, that explained that. It also seemed everyone was related to everyone else, which George guessed should have come as no surprise.

The high point of the evening was when Qapin proposed the toast. "To our Chief Engineer: we look forward to your repairing our systems."

Blazing pain knocked George right out of his seat and he heard and echoing voice in his mind, *You must come to me! Come to the Empire! Brook no delay!*

George blinked rapidly as Greth and Lawson tried to help him up. Mendra shouted for everyone to get out of her way.

"I'm fine," he muttered as he blinked back the afterimage of a silver haired man with pointed ears.

George rose to his feet with the help of Greth and Lawson, and felt compelled to leave at once. Drowsily, George said, "I can't stay."

"What do you mean you can't stay?" Qapin asked.

"Apparently, my ride home is waiting."

"Your what?" he said.

"Sorry, old figure of speech, which apparently was lost on your ancestral voyage here."

Lawson said, "But, George, you can't go. You've so much to teach us, to teach me."

"The Core can do that now that it's in phase with you. Just use the uplink."

"Where will you go?" Mendra asked.

He pointed east. "Thataway."

"But, George, the Core doesn't recognize us as crew as it does you."

'He has an excellent point there, George.' Staff quipped.

"That's easy," George assured. The staff flared in his hand as he linked with the ship's computer.

"Additions to the crew directory," George called.

STANDING BY.

"Lawson, Assistant Chief Engineer," he announced as the dwarf troll suddenly grinned.

ACKNOWLEDGED.

"Mendra, Chief Medical Officer."

ACKNOWLEDGED.

"Qapin is now second in command of the ship," which apparently was the highest captaincy rank allowed since the ship still recognized its senior captain as "location undetermined."

ACKNOWLEDGED.

"Greth is colonel of the ship's marine detachment."

ACKNOWLEDGED.

"Councilor Berrick is barred from attaining crew status as the Head of the Ship's Archives and all his current staff members until such time as, I, as senior officer rescinds this order."

ACKNOWLEDGED.

"You will assist the designated crewmembers and those they so designate in education and repair of systems, noting that system functions may have to be tested, even if they should, according to all known laws of science, be inoperable."

ACKNOWLEDGED.

"Chief Engineer, George Bradley, out." Staff's glow dimmed as everyone stood proudly.

He felt a twinge of a headache coming on as he added, "With that taken care of, I can be on my way tomorrow." The headache quickly faded.

'George, that was weird.'

"You're telling me," he said under his breath and smiled at his new friends.

"What does colonel of marines mean?" Greth said.

"Look it up, you're gonna love it."

Cle'or was giving George the oddest look at that point in his story. Se'and remained impossible to read. Her mind never leaked a thought either, George realized, as opposed to Fri'il whose thoughts bordered on hero worship.

No, not good at all, he thought.

'Maybe you'll get lucky, George.'

He coughed and glared at his staff.

'George! I meant maybe she'll fall for Balfour.'

Now the elfblooded Balfour coughed, obviously overhearing that last mental remark. He whispered, "You do realize I'm a lot older than you?"

George smiled. Balfour looked about twenty-six, making George the older in appearance.

"But that story doesn't explain the blade," Se'and said.

"Or your wyvern cloak," said Me'oh.

"No, it doesn't, does it?"

"Come on, Je'orj, please tell us," Se'and asked. Her being the first to ask surprised George.

"Please," Fri'il said.

"Oh, all right."

"George, your ugly face has grown on me."

"Thanks, Mendra."

She smiled, "I made this for you. We don't want you to catch cold out there." She presented him with a folded cloak which caught the light in such a way that he had difficulty looking at it.

"Go on, put it on."

George wrapped himself in the heavy cloak.

"It's from the wyvern that tried to kill you in Ashra Kodiu. It only seemed fitting since we wrapped your staff in it so we could handle it when you were unconscious, that the rest be worn by you."

"Uh, thanks," George said, not really wanting to reflect on those details.

Greth drew his knife from his belt, "You will need this."

George looked at the blade's discolored metal, nearly black. "This isn't steel."

"It's an alloy that magery can't harm."

"You make it?"

"It is our greatest secret. Please ask no more about it."

"All right, thank you."

Qapin said, "When you face magery, that blade will sunder it. It can even rend spells cast against you. Keep it with you, always!"

"I will, I promise."

"The giving of a knife," Greth said, "also means we are blood brothers."

"Does that me you want me to cut myself with it?"

"Cut yourself? No, please do not. Being of the blood of humans has been sacrifice enough for our people."

George nodded, looking up at him. His eyes were so kind for a troll out of a nightmare. "I will lead you to our border. It is best to go soon before the others realize their chief engineer has left without doing any more great miracles."

He looked about, "What of Lawson?"

"Lawson," Qapin said. "That young man doesn't want you to go."

Mendra said, "What's worse is he wants to go with you."

"I don't think it would be wise," George said.

"It wouldn't be," Qapin agreed, "he's Assistant Chief Engineer and has much to learn from the Core. He will have much to teach us, I have no doubt."

"Who would have thought those who are ugliest could be so important to our People?" Mendra asked.

George simply nodded.

Greth led him out through the warren of long abandoned corridors, when they heard the sound of running feet. Greth drew his knife, then saw it was Lawson and put it away. "How did you find us?"

"The Core's re-routed Internal Security. I could see you on the monitors."

"You're doing well with the systems, then."

"Core's begun teaching me and it wants me to teach the younger children while they are still small enough to wear the uplink helmets. It's got two more terminals running on the upper level so I can keep them out of the Core."

"That's great, Lawson."

"You know I want to come with you," Lawson admitted to George.

"You can't."

"Yet."

"Lawson," Greth rasped.

Lawson smiled, "You watch for me. I'll find you! We engineers gotta stick together!"

George gave him a hug, which was easier to do than the awkward one he had given to the crying Mendra, who was nearly ten feet tall. "Study hard, my friend, and encourage those kids to as well. Prect needs more like you."

"Don't go," Lawson whispered.

"I have to. It's my only chance of getting back home."

Lawson stepped back and jabbed his finger at Greth, "You take beyond the border!"

"I'll take him as far as I can."

Greth turned the manual hatch and opened the door to the outside world where the sunlight was bright. All George could see for miles was sand stretching to the horizon. He glanced back at Lawson and felt a mental tugging and heard a quiet voice, *Come. Come to the Empire.*

George stood up and stretched.

"You can't just end the tale there, Je'orj!" Fri'il pleaded.

"Oh, yes, I can," he laughed.

"Balfour's told us about his nephew, Casber, seeing you battling in the Great Waste."

"What? Oh, that was nothing."

Cle'or probed, "You fought more wyverns, didn't you?"

"An army of them! So, I really don't need your help."

Se'and shook her head, "You're a terrible liar! That whole tale was a lie, wasn't it? Living with trolls, bah!"

George watched her stalk off, while Fri'il looked at him, then glanced at Se'and's retreating back.

Cle'or said, "We have wasted enough time. If we push the horses we should be able to reach Edous before dusk."

"You'll like Edous," Balfour said. "It's a decent sized city-state, although a tad boring."

"I can do with boring," George said.

'Se'and's kinda cute when she's mad.'

George leaned on his staff and muttered, "Shut up."

Fri'il frowned, "What?"

"Uh, nothing, just thinking aloud."

'She's cute, too.'

"Shut up."

Fri'il glanced back as Balfour struggled to not laugh.

Me'oh brought over salve, "George, this should help with those saddle sores. Could you use any help with it?"

"No!"

Balfour fell down laughing. Staff, at least, had the grace to keep its mechanical thoughts to itself.

Chapter 12: The Inn

The acolyte ran up the steps past the gleaming stone columns of the ebone rock used to build the Temple. The structure dwarfed the other buildings lining the square.

The black-robed priest he reported to was skeptical, but allowed him to proceed. The young acolyte had the merest trace of elvin blood, but it was enough to wield magery. He bowed low, entering the study of the woman with long flowing black hair, her black robes silken. "High Priestess, I am honored!"

"Speak quickly and do not waste my time!" she rasped as she fed her pet, a black-furred beast rising on its haunches and growling at the acolyte. The creature shimmered and transformed into a large black feathered bird, squawked and leapt to its perch, eyeing the acolyte hungrily.

"I bring a warning, mistress! A new power has entered the city!" he shouted.

"Bah!" she exclaimed as the bird fanned its wings. "I would have felt such a thing! You waste my time!" Raising her hands, she began to cast a spell that would teach the lowly acolyte a lesson he would not soon forget.

The acolyte shrilled, "Please listen to me, mistress!"

She relented and altered the spell. The acolyte trembled as he felt the force of her magery build around him, then settle within. He stiffened, thinking back to the arrival of the strangers. She saw them in his memory with acuity far beyond mortal seeing.

He had first seen the elvin half-breed dressed in mountain furs. Only the faintest aura of the gift clung about him. His was clearly a paltry gift that might best manifest a weak skill for healing, something even the acolyte could not mistake for a major power.

He had observed the other members of the party, all human. The sight of the black cloaked Cathartan escort was curious. What errand for their sire would bring such people here so far from their cursed land?

Perhaps they bore a bespelled charm or talisman? The acolyte's memory focused on the human male with a staff tethered by his

93

knee.

He was rather strangely dressed. His tunic and pants were of an unusual fabric and color. The acolyte noticed the faintest aura of magery about him. It was instantly clear that the man had no trace of elvin blood, no inborn mage talent. Abruptly, that very impression vanished, making the acolyte wonder if he had really seen anything at all.

The staff suddenly drew the acolyte's attention, he recalled. It briefly glowed with an immense aura of power. That must be the source of the magery. A mage's staff lay in the hands of a human!

The High Priestess returned to the present, aghast. That staff blazed in her mind with the purest power. It was disguised by a powerful spell that must have been forgotten in all but the oldest of Elvin Lore.

"I must have it!" she shrieked. She shouted for her gray robed servitors, old human males long sworn to her dark master.

They hurried to her from the adjoining room and quickly removed the acolyte's wilted body. They did their best to avoid looking at the burned cinders that had been his eyes. As they carried him away, the dark bird squawked, straining to reach the fresh meat.

"Oh, not for you, my sweet," she laughed, "soon you'll feast upon a foolish human who fancies himself a mage!"

George tried not to gawk as they rode through the city of Edous. All thought of his saddle sores and the pains of actually riding a horse were forgotten. The city was incredible. Narrow streets filled with people hocking wares. A mother glanced out her second story window, saw their escort, then shouted to her children to come inside. The woman's fear was much less interesting than the window's wooden shutters beside her. He marveled at the intricate workmanship and skill.

Ox drawn carts laden with produce halted for them as they passed, while his black cloaked escort smiled thinly as they watched the crowds. He felt as if he had gone back in time and was glimpsing an ancient city out of the Middle Ages. It was an archaeologist's dream. Yet, in truth it was this particular archaeologist's nightmare.

They reached their destination and the youngest member of his Cathartan escort, Fri'il, hurriedly dismounted and rushed to help him. Less awkwardly than he imagined, he got off the horse. She looked at him as if in reproach and took the reins.

He groaned, wishing he could have found some way to turn down the unwanted gift of their four member escort. The women had ignored their offer of release from service. As far as they were concerned, Sire Ryff's lifebond to serve and protect them was inviolate.

George's musings were driven from his thoughts as Balfour reached the door to the inn and spoke to Se'and, the nominal leader of their escort.

"I'll handle this," he assured.

She looked at him condescendingly. "Master, I'm quite experienced in these matters. But, if you would like to make our arrangements, please do."

George, frustrated, explained, "I would like to get some rest, so if we could just get on with it, I would appreciate it."

Se'and straightened and bowed, then held the door for them to enter.

"M'lord Je'orj," she whispered, "you do not yet comprehend the honor my sire has granted you both."

"That's, doubtless, true," he replied.

"Welcome to Edous!" an old innkeeper greeted. He suspiciously eyed Balfour in his mountain garb. "It is you, master Winome. It has been some time since last you passed this way. But surely you are a healer by now."

Balfour winced. Years before he had come through Edous on his way to the Imperial Healer's Hall in the Aqwaine Empire. He smiled, putting aside the memories of his failure. Things were different now that he was George's protégé.

The innkeeper nodded at the elfblood's companions.

"How may I serve you, Master Winome?"

"We are a party of six and seek suitable lodgings for the night. Preferably two rooms and an adjoining bath," the young elfblood added, glancing at his companion, who could not quite hide his saddle induced limp.

A pained look crossed the innkeeper's face. "I'm so sorry. But I've no such available. Perhaps you might care for space here in the common room?"

Balfour opened his mouth to protest, when Se'and abruptly confronted the man.

"That will simply not do, sir. We are a Cathartan Household and must have private accommodations suitable to our station. We will take your best rooms for a fair remuneration, of course."

The innkeeper smiled and cleared his throat.

Piqued, Balfour was ready to interject as George placed a restraining hand on his arm. He sighed as Se'and smiled thinly. The innkeeper named the price, to which she responded, "That's a price for a room in the Empire, but here in the Crescent?"

He protested.

She raised her hand, "Does not Cathartan gold still bring higher value in the exchange?" She jingled her weighty purse.

Greed gleamed in his eyes. "Say a gold per suite, per day?"

She chuckled. "Let's see the rooms first just to be certain they a worth such a price."

With a clap of his hands, the innkeeper grinned. "Right this way, my lady."

The innkeeper brought them to a hall of vacant, mid-sized rooms, none impressive to George but suitable enough to rest in. They looked upon a simple room with a wide bed and a small window overlooking the street.

"Balfour and I will take this room, you and the others may take another," George commented casually after the innkeeper left with Se'and's gold for the night's lodging in his hands.

Se'and simply smiled at George and shook her head, following him into the room. "I stay with you as is my duty. Me'oh will join Master Balfour in the other."

The elfblood healer glanced behind him as Me'oh took his bag to the other room. She paused, waiting for the elfblood at the door.

"My lord?"

Balfour swallowed and glanced at George helplessly, then noted the same look on his friend's face. Se'and, in the meantime, set their bags down defiantly.

"This is not necessary," George stated, already knowing such protest was futile. "I am quite capable of protecting myself."

"That's debatable, but not the issue, M'lord," she said as she closed the door. She had picked up calling him "M'lord" again. "We have our duties to perform and it is best you come to accept our role," she added, assessing the large single bed in the room.

George cleared his throat and leaned heavily on his staff, "This is not Cathart, Se'and. Men are not an endangered species as they are in your land. We don't need to be protected at the cost of your very lives."

Se'and shook her head. "Accept that we are yours, body and soul. We are a Cathartan house by bond at my sire's word. There can be no higher responsibility."

"You know what I intend," he said, even at that moment feeling the inexplicable pull westward. "You know what I must do."

"You are Summoned," she replied, having seen the impact of the spell take its physical toll on him. "We will accompany you to the Empire and help you find the answers you seek. But understand we intend to do our duty."

He could hear the pleading note that underscored her words. "Understand and respect that and matters will be much simpler."

He moved across the room and gazed out the window. His protests were, indeed, futile, while she could not understand the distance between them.

Viewing the city from this vantage, he slowly closed his eyes and concentrated, opening himself to rapport. As Se'and watched him standing there, his staff began to glow. The disguising wooden image grew faint, revealing the scaled wyvern hide insulating it that lent the staff its camouflage. The crystal staff's glow danced in response to George's thoughts.

The city rose before him in his mind's eye. Lines formed, creating a map in relief. The true details of the city's foundation, hidden beneath grime and myriad structures, formed. The only difference between this visioning and so many others he had had over the years was that this site was not an ancient ruin needing painstaking extrapolation. This was a place that should exist only in the much vaunted past, not his here and now. His consciousness expanded outward, touching the reality that was the city-state of Edous. He did not belong here; wherever here was in the cosmos.

"This isn't even my world!" he said breaking rapport, opening his eyes wide.

Se'and frowned at how forlorn he looked, the staff once more appearing to be a thing of wood.

"An even better reason to trust my judgment, M'lord."

Sighing, he heard the door open and could see Fri'il and the fierce looking Cle'or, with their baggage in hand, talking heatedly about something. Se'and fought hard not to laugh at George's puzzled expression. Abruptly the conversation ended. Fri'il hefted her bags and entered their room with a sheepish glance at the staring George.

"What was that all about?" he muttered as Fri'il secured the door behind her.

Smiling broadly, Se'and shook her head as Fri'il blushed and headed toward the adjoining bath chamber and said, "I'll see to your bath, M'lord."

"Fri'il, set those over there, your sleeping mat is on the floor there. Then see to it that dinner is sent up."

The two women left him alone while the staff in his hand sparkled, remarking something unheard to everyone but George. He scoffed and mumbled back to it, "Oh, just mind your own business."

Chapter 13: Lord Je'orj Being Difficult

Steam rose from the tub as George lowered himself, gingerly. He sighed as the hot water soothed his aches. Picking up a bar of sweet smelling soap he began scrubbing the dirt from his skin. After a while, he sat back and took a moment to luxuriate in the peace and quiet.

Abruptly, Se'and and Fri'il entered the chamber, wearing only their bodices and sleek knives strapped to their legs. Embarrassed he ordered them out. They smiled back as Se'and grabbed a bar of soap and Fri'il moved behind him to massage his shoulders.

George hastily tried to launch himself out of the tub, then quickly thought better of the idea and hurriedly covered his privates. With a thin lipped smile, Se'and started rubbing soap into his hair. Swallowing angrily, thinking enough was enough, he shut his eyes tight and concentrated, then mentally "pushed" the two grinning women away.

Shoved roughly backward, the women steeled themselves for the fight. They had expected and prepared themselves for his magely trickery. Se'and took a firm grip of his hair, and held on for dear life while Fri'il dug her fingers into his shoulders, putting painful pressure on his nerves. The force exerted against them suddenly eased as George grunted in pain.

Grinning, Se'and asked, "Going to behave yourself?"

He turned his head and glared at her.

"You will let us do this properly," she asserted, and yanked on his hair for good measure.

He gazed up at the ceiling and realized he had dropped the soap. Sighing, he acquiesced.

Fri'il gently massaged his neck and back as Se'and took great pleasure in working out the tangles in his hair.

Finally, finishing their ministrations, they left the chamber. Gratefully, he rose halfway from the tub then paused, looking about for the towel. He was certain that it was near a moment ago, then noticed that his clothes were gone as well.

During his momentary confusion, Se'and and Fri'il burst back into the room with the towels to dry him. He gaped, stunned as the two now naked women dried him thoroughly before ushering him out. Each gave him a quick kiss on the cheek for his good behavior.

He glanced back as Se'and got into the tub, while Fri'il added more hot water from the stove before helping wash her hair. He left one of the towels behind as he struggled to think about something else, anything else.

It was bad enough, George thought, *that to get home I must follow the Summoning's lead. I'm not going to let them mess with me, demanding I play a role in this marriage-by-bond tradition.*

Me'oh had since taken up guard duty. She asked him if she could help him dress for bed. He simply stared back at her then said, "No, thank you."

She grinned, "You will learn to appreciate our ways."

I hope not, he fervently wished. He wanted to get off this world and back home. He swallowed hard and asked Me'oh to turn around. He wanted some dignity.

The streets cleared as grey-robed acolytes of the temple appeared in the quarter. They began surrounding the inn. The city guard then decided to patrol another district. Sight of the acolytes also caused the quick barring of windows. When all was quiet, the black-robed priests and the High Priestess of the Lord of Demons, herself, approached, accompanied by her shape-changed and now dark furred hellhound.

She motioned to her minions, who flocked to her. "I want them all dead and the staff brought directly to me. My pet is only to be used should any of you fail me."

The acolytes paled. "We will not fail!" they averred.

Her smile chilled them as she waved them away while a half dozen of her priests remained by her side. "The human will see what true power is just before he dies." She chuckled, knowing that soon the staff would be hers.

George slept fitfully with Se'and resting soundly beside him. Sweat gleamed across his brow as he fought in the thrall of a familiar nightmare. He dreamt of standing at the dig, examining the two peculiar stones that had apparently served as the base for an arch, then falling, seemingly forever. He relived the fight with the wyverns and the outcome in his nightmare was the same as in his waking life. To relive it as it happened was terrifying all the same.

'George, wake up, your heart and respiratory rates are dangerously elevated. Recommend entering primary rapport mode.'

Se'and was shaking him as he opened his eyes and whispered, "You were shaking and crying out. Are you all right?" Fri'il rose hurriedly from her sleeping mat.

Se'and frowned as he merely muttered, "Report."

'You seem to have had a powerful stimulus from the Summoning.' The probability is high that it is a warning. Alert status is advised.'

George glanced at the softly glowing staff leaning against the headboard. Fri'il and Se'and were looking at him in concern as they saw him nod and mutter, "Scan and wake Balfour. I fear we may not have much time."

"M'lord?" said Se'and.

The staff flared and the scan swept through the building and the outside environs. He smiled grimly, "We've company coming, ladies."

That said, he hefted the now brightly glowing staff across his lap, which muted the light it cast.

"Robbers?" Se'and questioned, shaking her head.

"Not common ones, if they are. They seem to have magical assistance from the feel of it. Fri'il, back your sleeping mat away from the door and take a position over there."

The staff flared with brilliant light as Fri'il moved to her new post and drew her short sword. They all grew quiet and watched the door. Se'and poised on her knees atop the bed, her bodice's drawstrings still loosened for sleep. A bead of sweat dropped from George's brow as he deepened rapport with his computer staff. More and more functions were taken up by the recesses of his mind as the staff's glow dimmed to the light of a burning ember.

George whispered to Se'and, "We wouldn't want our friends to know they are expected."

After a time, the floorboards outside began to creak underfoot.

There was an abrupt hush outside, then red fire engulfed the door and it burst asunder. Fiery splinters rained across the room. For a moment, Fri'il was forced to shield her eyes as the first grey-robed figures rushed inside, silhouetted by the smoke and flame.

Se'and drew and cast two of her daggers into the smoke, even as George hissed, "Don't kill them!"

"Will they do less?" she hotly replied as her victims fell back wounded.

"Don't kill!" he demanded even as cries of pain could be heard from the other suite.

The red fire that had shattered the door gathered itself, while George hastily peeled back the disguising leathery hide from the tip of his staff. Revealed was pure glowing white crystal, which surprised Se'and. George grimly looked at the balled fire which now hovered above the remains of the shattered door, then used the pent up force he had stabled in his mind and sent a pure bolt of white fire into the magical force rising against him.

The explosion was deafening to the grey-robed minions seeking to charge into the room behind the dark force. They were knocked backward into the hallway, unconscious. A blast of purest malevolent intent abruptly shot into the room as a black-robed figure strode through the doorway.

White fire flared from George's staff and deflected the blast. The figure cupped his hands and red energy welled as he readied another attack.

Fri'il cast a dagger at him as she moved to put herself between her lord and harm. "No!" George shouted even as the black-robed mage chanted an incantation.

Her dagger slowed in midair as George leapt forward and grabbed the young woman backward with one arm. The black-robed figure's chant ended as the dagger stopped and spun back toward Fri'il.

Energy flashed from the blazing crystal staff, blasting the dagger as George fell backward onto the bed with Fri'il struggling in his arm, desperate to defend him. A ball of energy shot from the priest's hands and was upon them. There was a terrible flash of light and an explosion.

The resultant blast shook the very walls.

Staff's shrill warning had awakened Balfour. He woke Me'oh and Cle'or and alerted them to danger. In the melee that soon began, Cle'or fought their attackers with unmatched fury, her sword a blur of motion.

The legendary skill of Cathartan swordswomen was revealed to be no mere boast to the acolytes, who dodged back out of the room. One cried out to someone yet to be revealed as the window overlooking the balcony shattered. A black-robed figure stood there with hands raised, chanting. Me'oh threw one of her daggers, which bounced off him.

Hearing the spell forming, Balfour concentrated and without uttering a single bespelled word reached out with his gift. Stretching out his hand, he lightly touched thumb to forefinger and the black-robed figure, whom he recognized as a servant of the Demonlord, staggered, clutching at his throat, the spell forgotten as he struggled to breathe. He desperately gasped out the final words of his spell and Balfour's bed burst into flame.

Cle'or ignored the distraction to pursue her attack, forcing the last gray-robed minions back. They shouted for help and the sound of running feet confirmed reinforcements a certainty. Me'oh pushed Balfour back into a corner, holding her sword poised for defense as Cle'or readied herself.

Still without uttering a spell, Balfour gazed at the burning bed and concentrated his will. The flames were smothered, suddenly starved of the oxygen upon which they fed. The gasping dark-robed priest stared in astonishment, one echoed by the circle of priests working in concert with the High Priestess below, whose combined strength powered the dark spells being used this night.

With the last of his strength, a bolt of energy blasted from the choking priest's hand and arched toward the elfblood. Balfour tried to ward it yet knew it was futile, even as he released his mental hold on the mageborn's windpipe. The dark figure sank to his knees and sucked for breath.

Cle'or grimaced and leapt between the blast and its target, even as Balfour concentrated on deflecting it. It veered minutely from its deadly course and glanced off Cle'or.

Her shoulder and arm were outlined in red ethereal fire, taking the partial blow. The rest struck the wall deafeningly, only inches to Balfour's right.

The mageborn eyed him darkly as he rose once more, but this time Balfour was without mercy, believing Cle'or dead. He gestured once more and the black-robed figure clutched his chest as his heart ceased to beat. He fell backward and faded out of existence.

The acolytes who had appeared in the doorway saw the vanishing and fled. An explosion from the next room echoed through the hall.

The priests' deaths reverberated through their circle's link. At the death of the first priest at the elfblood's hands, they had hurriedly sundered their tie before taking the full brunt of his agony. But this second demise had come too soon after the first and caught them totally unprepared. Never had they seen a spell work so fast or thoroughly.

The High Priestess swayed elsewhere, images dancing in her mind. One priest felled, his heart crushed by the young elfblood's ethereal grip; another dead moments after the explosion. The latter's last glance showed to those bound to her circle that which should have been impossible; the man with his staff yet lived.

One moment, the human was destined for death by their combined might, and in the next, triumphant. In sympathetic reaction, one of her priests clutched his face, feeling the terrible burns their colleague had suffered as if they were his own. In shock, the High Priestess realized that she had grossly underestimated her opponents. In her recklessness she had not recognized that the man must have a strong tie of elvin blood and that his companion must be a mage as well, one who had somehow cleverly concealed the breadth of his gifts.

However, all was not lost. She shouted an order to release her beast. "My pet! Kill the human mage and bring me his staff!" The creature bounded toward the building as her dazed acolytes hastily moved out of its way.

"Focus!" she screamed at her priests, calling the circle back to its work.

Chapter 14: Inn the Worse for Were

From the cellar doorway, the innkeeper cautiously peered and hushed those behind him who had sought refuge in the now invaded inn.

At the sight of the beast loping past, he blanched, then noticed a temple acolyte slumped unconscious on the floor, at least he hoped he was only unconscious as he shut the door tight.

The beast did not pause as it bounded toward the stairway to the second floor. A wounded acolyte was midway down the stairs and saw the beast too late. He was casually swatted aside as it raced past. The acolyte struggled back to his feet, thankful to be alive and limped away as fast as he could, desperate to escape knowing what the beast's entry boded.

Smoke wafted from the ruins of the suite's entry; where the doorway had stood only a great jagged hole remained. The beast slowed to sniff the air. Its eyes glowed with red fire as it padded forward and entered the room.

Only one piece of furniture lay unscathed by the damage: the bed. Upon it lay a young woman who was barely conscious, and beside her another woman watched warily, sword upraised. The man, his true prey, stood next to the bed, turning away from the stricken woman.

The man instantly became the sole focus of the beast's attention.

The staff! its mistress's voice urged in its mind. *I must have the staff! Bring it to me!*

The man frowned almost as if he could hear the unspoken words. He faced it squarely, holding the glowing staff. The beast took another step closer and white light flared around it repelling it. It charged back, undaunted.

The defensive field George had erected flared once more and the dark beast cried out in pain as it was flung backward. It shook itself as it rose and started to pace the dazzling perimeter while periodically glancing at them.

With startling swiftness it again charged and struck his force field. White fire silhouetted the animal as it willed itself beyond the pain. To George's horror, he realized that the beast would soon penetrate the shield. He had to act quickly.

"Se'and, hold me!" he shouted.

He sat back down on the edge of the bed, gripping the now brightly blazing staff in his hands then slumped, unconscious. Se'and dropped her short sword to the bed in her haste to grab him up.

The barrier flared suddenly so bright that the walls of the room seemed almost transparent, unable to contain the light. Shrieking in indescribable agony, the beast lost its chosen shape, abruptly transitioning into a dark bird of the same proportions. In vain it tried to fly above the barrier entrapping it to dive upon its victims from above.

The bird's searing pain backlashed through the High Priestess' circle, choking off the chants they used to maintain focus and add their power to her creature's. They cried out in stinging agony.

George, his mind free of his physical body, so deeply enrapport with his staff, found himself able to "glimpse" the elvin woman who served to focus the creature's thoughts. He could hear her mutter, "Fools!"

He felt her pour every ounce of her will into strengthening the creature's attack. The bird's wings beat stronger, raising it gradually higher toward the ceiling within his flaring defensive field of energy.

'Yes! Higher still!' the Priestess shrilled, seeing through her creature's eyes. *'Kill the humans and bring me the staff!'*

The strain of the rapport was taking its toll; George's respiration became ragged. He knew he could not keep this up much longer. There was only one thing he could do. He dropped the barrier and the bird abruptly flew over them.

Fri'il, awakening more fully, reacted to the great bird preparing to attack them hastily grabbing the fallen weapon beside her. Se'and threw herself across their lord's vulnerable body, even as the staff he held rigidly in his grasp fired a blast of light.

With but a single squawk the bird fell helplessly to the floor with a terrible thud. Its body shivered as George groaned. Se'and shook him, "Je'orj! Please wake up!"

His eyes opened faintly. She gasped, seeing not human eyes, but those of a bird.

George found himself elsewhere, his staff glowing wanly in his hands. He looked about carefully and concluded he was standing in a spell-enwrapped web. Thick strands clung to everything around him. This was not at all what he had expected. At this moment, he should have been one with the shape-changing creature's every thought, not disassociated from it.

He could sense the were-bird's convulsions. Curious, he pushed past the nearest strands that blocked his path. His progress was slowed as the web drew tighter before him until finally he reached a solidly woven wall of strands. Using his staff as a torch, he peered more closely and discovered there were faintly glowing elvin runes. The characters shimmered with the were's life energy and will.

George swung the staff high over his head then struck the entwined strands with all his might. The were-bird went rigid with shock and George paled as the world around him quaked and a scream of rage echoed around him. He smiled grimly, knowing he had succeeded. The runes here no longer functioned as intended. The were was no longer without free will.

Exhaustedly, George closed his eyes and hoped he had not been away from his physical body for too long.

Cle'or gasped in pain on the floor beside Balfour. He knelt and closed his eyes in concentration as Me'oh stood over them defensively. Reaching out with his senses, he probed the deep burns on Cle'or's shoulder and upper arm. She was in excruciating pain. He dealt with that first, deeply concentrating. She moaned with relief as her pain abruptly eased.

Accessing the injury further, he focused on redirected the flow of blood then repaired the damage to her blood vessels. The healing process was slow; he dared not hurry. Since apprenticing to George, his training had relied on Staff's knowledge and ability to augment his talent. Precious minutes passed. The burns slowly faded and the flesh became whole once more. Balfour leaned back against the wall and sighed, clearly exhausted.

Cle'or blinked her eyes wearily and glanced at her former injury, seeing pink skin where the burn should have been a raw wound.

"The others. We must go to them."

Me'oh glanced at Balfour, "Are you strong enough to bring her, M'lord?"

"Give me a moment," he muttered as he mentally reached out to George and his staff, but found himself blocked. He struggled to help Cle'or to her feet, knowing something was desperately wrong in the next room. Me'oh cautiously led the way.

George awoke, feeling half frozen. He realized that he was lying upon the bed, buried beneath layers of blankets. He was not alone. Two bodies clung about him, sharing their warmth.

Noticing he was awake first, Fri'il clung tighter and exclaimed, "Thank the Lords!"

Se'and breathed a sigh of relief. Tears in her eyes, she leaned closer, kissed him, then shouted, "Don't do that again! We thought you were dead!"

Fri'il turned her head and looked over her shoulder, "Master Balfour, it's working!"

"Can't a person get any bloody sleep around here?" he replied blearily, propped up in a chair Me'oh brought from another room.

"Do try to be quiet, all of you," Me'oh said as she rose from her post by the remains of the doorway. "Cle'or needs to rest and that bed, doubtless, cannot take much more strain."

George glanced past Se'and and noticed the prone form beside her, then lay back and muttered through numbed lips, "Report."

Your respiration is increasing to normal levels, heart rate is still weak, but improving. Monitoring functions were temporarily suspended due to the depth of our rapport. Passive conscious memory indicates that Balfour authorized current emergency revival methods. No long term damage indicated.'

"Status of our new friend, here?" he asked the computer.

'Unconscious. A state I am maintaining through the link we forged. Balfour has been checking it as well at intervals. He concludes that there is no danger of the creature awakening. All outside links to the will of its former master have been severed; although, it is still bound by enchantment.'

Fri'il rose and poured a glass of water, then urged George to take a few sips. It soothed his parched lips. She had to hold it for him ever so gently. He laid his head back exhaustedly, wishing he could untangle himself from his two caretakers as Fri'il set the glass aside and snuggled close. Her thoughts were dark. She had trouble understanding this man that she had been bonded to by Se'and's brother, Vyss, who had originally been intended to be her husband.

They effectively held him pinned between them and there was nothing he could do about it.

Through his rapport, Staff commented, *'These are not particularly unpleasant sensations.'*

George sighed, wishing that when he had fallen into this world he had not been clutching the computer staff quite so hard.

'I heard that.'

Yet beyond his vengeful humor, his condition frightened him more than he dared to consider. George had never imagined the reality of going so deeply into rapport that the computer would have been unable to monitor his physical condition, superseded by his total absorption with other matters. He cleared his throat and asked what had happened.

Se'and uncharacteristically buried her face against him, sharing Fri'il's concerned look as he weakly muttered to himself in two timbres as if two people were talking to one another. Fri'il glanced at Balfour as he knelt to examine George.

The elfblood smiled, "No need to worry. I know both of them well enough to know everything is all right when Staff needles him like that."

Fri'il glanced at the wanly glowing staff, her lord still terribly cold to the touch. She wondered if she had chosen wisely. She could not forget the moment he had pulled her backward, preventing her attempt to protect him from the dark mage's sorcery.

Perhaps, she wondered, *I would have been better off choosing to bond the elfblood.*

It was darkest night when Cle'or awoke in surprise. She vaguely saw Fri'il rise from the bed off to her right. The young woman glanced back at her deeply sleeping lord, then put on her livery, checked her weapons and crossed the room.

Faint light lit the hall, where Me'oh stood on guard. The older woman turned as Cle'or rose and in startled realization touched her upper arm. Her bodice had been burned away at the shoulder and her skin felt incredibly tender but no more.

Me'oh whispered, "Sister, rest, all is well."

Yet she rose nonetheless, too quickly and her head pounded, her headache slowly abating.

Me'oh came over to her. "Have you scouted the building?"

"No, I've dared not leave all of you alone like this. I've heard no sound of movement in the inn, either. I think us safe enough."

Cle'or looked about and saw her weapons. She knelt, donned her livery and strapped her weapons about her. She unsheathed a dagger and pushed past Me'oh, who moved to delay her. However, the older woman recognized the look in Cle'or's eyes and knew it would be no use.

"You need rest!" Balfour rasped as he stirred, then hurried over to them.

Cle'or glared back at him and touched her shoulder, "Why did you heal me so?"

He frowned, not understanding.

Exasperated, she stated, "I am a House Champion. I've earned many scars, yet healing me like this? You dishonor me!"

Angrily, Balfour responded, "You could have lost use of that arm, then what kind of champion would you have been?"

"One who bore an honorable disfigurement earned in trying to protect her ungrateful lord's life!" He was left speechless, and she brushed past him and out of the room.

Fri'il moved out of her way and glanced at Me'oh, who whispered to Balfour, "Should there be a next time, leave her a scar."

Cle'or warily explored the hallway. The only sign of their attackers had been a burned piece of dark fabric, not unlike that worn by the mage that had attacked them. She went cautiously down the stairs.

The inn seemed abandoned. She glanced out one of the windows and noticed that there was no sound of dogs or evidence that anyone had come to investigate what had happened. That bespoke either a powerful spell, fear, or perhaps both. She headed toward the kitchen. Pots and pans were strewn upon the floor. She paused to take a much-needed deep breath, momentarily feeling dizzy, and noted the cellar door. She crept closer and tried the knob. Finding it locked, she eased her dagger blade between the jam and unbarred the door.

The faint light of the kitchen revealed bleary-eyed frightened faces. She recognized one and smiled, "Innkeeper, our rooms are in need of some airing out."

He stared up at her as if she were an apparition and fainted.

The innkeeper hesitantly came up the stairs with Cle'or, holding a lantern. The portly man looked at the damage and destruction with growing horror. "My inn, my poor inn," he muttered. "How will I pay for all this?"

Balfour met him as he surveyed the room. "Was anyone with you hurt?"

"Hurt? No, no, when the first acolytes appeared, the guests and my staff fled with me to the only safe place I could think of. There, in the cellar."

"Acolytes?"

The innkeeper shivered, "From the Dark Temple."

Staring at him, Balfour gasped.

George opened his eyes and thought at his companion. Who are they?

Balfour thought back. A cult to the Demonlord, He Who Dwells In The North.

George thought about that, having a sinking feeling as he realized the presence of the cult in these human lands boded ill. The nightmare that had awoken him now made greater sense. The Summoning had been trying to warn him.

"Has the city gone mad to raise a temple to the Elfking?" Balfour rasped.

Lowering his head, the innkeeper replied, "Our city has fallen on dark times. The elvin witch who is their master came here only a few years ago. She promised prosperity and used her magery to help many. Those with the merest elvin blood flocked to her. The temple has risen in power ever since." The innkeeper noticed the stilled bird lying on the floor and hastened to flee the room.

Cle'or grabbed him from behind and put a knife to his throat. The innkeeper felt as if he were going to faint once more. "Now, now," she whispered in his ear.

"How? How have you done this?" he cried. "We have no mages who can defeat such as the witch and her minions!"

Balfour smiled grimly, "You do, now."

At that the innkeeper blinked in realization. "I must see the council. They must know of this. But it is useless; the inn is likely being watched."

Cle'or smiled. "Do not concern yourself about that."

The innkeeper glanced at her and roused his courage. It would not be easy, but he just might be able to notify his patron, Lord Gerig.

Back in the broken, still smoldering room, George awoke, feeling stronger and not quite as cold. He slowly tried to extricate himself from Se'and's sleeping embrace. She instantly awoke and gripped him painfully between the legs, then, to his complete shock, she kissed him.

He gasped and quickly learned his lesson. Staff chose wisely not to comment as he settled back unresisting.

She released him and whispered wryly, "My, you must really be feeling better."

He turned his face away from her and sighed. That took the grin off her face. This world offered him too much, and deep in his heart he knew he must return to his own. He would go to the Empire and find his way home.

Despite George's incessant explanations she did not understand and would not willingly understand. She shivered and huddled closer to this strange man that she was bound and pledged to protect, the core of her Cathartan house by bond.

It was too long a time before any of them fell asleep.

Chapter 15: Protecting an Unwilling Lord

Pale sunlight lit the room through the broken window. Balfour finished George's examination and said, "Take a hot bath, then I will decide if you are indeed hale and hearty."

Se'and had risen and dressed, spelling Fri'il at guard duty while Me'oh slept. The young woman removed her livery and made preparations in the adjoining room. Fri'il readied the tub as Cathartan tradition demanded. Once satisfied that the water was just right, she went back into the main room and announced, "Your bath is ready, M'lord," then offered to help him rise.

Acutely embarrassed, George asked for his cloak, which he used to robe himself. He felt dizzy as he accepted Fri'il's arm and left the room. She helped him into the steaming bath and, before he could protest, removed her bodice and offered to bathe him.

"Ah, no, that will be quite unnecessary, thank you. I'll be fine."

She paused then sat on the edge of the bath. "Do I displease you?"

He looked at the young woman in surprise. "No."

Sighing, she shook her head. "I do not understand your ways. I tried to defend you last night and you prevented me. You could have died doing what you did. Se'and and I helped save you! How is it you still do not see that you need us?"

George closed his eyes. "You don't understand," he muttered, feeling chilled once more even in the steaming bath. He could feel the Summoning stir. It so often drew him, forcing him to travel west, always toward the Empire. Yet this time it urged him to be here in this moment, to hold the young woman tight and embrace all this world offered. He felt conflicted, but knew he had to find a way off this world and quickly. He couldn't allow this world to claim his soul and his free will. She handed him the soap. He stared at it then sighed.

Staff bespoke him a few minutes later finishing his bath, rising from the tub as Fri'il handed him his towel and helped dry him off. He winced.

115

'George, sorry to disturb you, but Balfour wants to know what's taking you so long. I have told him. He says to tell you that in that case he certifies you now hale and hearty.'

In the adjacent room, the were's shape had softened. It no longer looked like a terrible bird of prey. It had become a falc, a keenly intelligent bird that was a legendary harbinger of change. Their group had already come across one such creature on their travels together and this worried Balfour to no end.

George dressed then approached the were-creature, staff in hand. Closing his eyes, he concentrated. The staff glowed brighter as the rapport deepened. The falc trembled and began to awaken, then shimmered and changed. They gaped.

"I've heard legends that speak of using a person's hair to create a binding, but never have I heard of anything like this," Balfour said as he knelt beside what was clearly forming into a girl, who looked to be about eleven years old.

Her hair was black and had grown so long that it was entwined about her body, so tightly woven that it covered her like a second skin. The girl looked up at them, clearly frightened. Se'and tried to smile, to comfort the child, who had plainly been held in the vilest of enchantments.

George slowly reached out and gently caressed the girl's cheek. He sought to discern her facial features wrapped in hair while allowing his staff to examine the bespelled patterns of the mask. His head began to ache at the complexity and the increased level of rapport the computer required.

"She is probably much older than she appears. Closer to Fri'il's age is my guess," Balfour offered. "I have no idea of how to break this enchantment."

Fri'il frowned, looking over George's shoulder, "What are you going to do?"

Se'and gave her a withering look, "They will do what must be done."

Nodding, George replied, "If there is anything to be done. If there is it must be done soon if we are to have any hope of not being interfered with."

"Unlikely, M'lord," Me'oh stated. "The Dark One, himself, will likely aid his Priesthood to prevent freeing its creature."

With a groan George said, "Let's hope not. Power of that nature would be rarely granted, if what Balfour's told me holds true. The Elfking may not even suspect that I survived crossing the Great Waste."

Se'and touched her dagger hilt and caught George's gaze, her meaning plain. He adamantly shook his head as he went to look through his things. George quickly found the strange blade of discolored metal and returned with it to kneel beside the girl. Me'oh, having seen it used before, shivered at the sight of it.

"You did not really get that in the Great Waste?" Fri'il muttered, stepping closer.

"It really was a gift from, ah, a very large friend as I've told you," he said.

Se'and shook her head in disbelief, "No one lives in the Waste any longer...other than the Dark One's ilk."

Balfour had once believed the same until George reached the Winome Clan on the Barrier Mountains, which overlooked that barren wasteland. The elfblood now believed a great many things that should have been impossible to credit.

"Is it enchanted?" Fri'il asked.

"Anything but," George replied. At the looks of incomprehension, he explained, "The alloy was developed to not be effected by elvin magery. It was a weapon used against Elfdom during the Great War between the human colony and the elves."

"But all human lore was lost at Battle's End, when mankind was defeated," Se'and said, remembering well the lessons she had learned at her Mother Shaman's knee.

"So say the legends of the peoples who fled the desolation and chaos. Consider, perhaps yours are not the only histories of mankind's last days before the birth of the new age." Those around

George shifted and frowned. Unwilling to say more and breach a confidence, he merely held up the strange blade.

"Well, this is worth a try, anyway. Balfour, please join me," he asked, then closed his eyes and mumbled to staff, "Monitor."

'Acknowledged.' In George's mind the patterns in the girl's hair were clearly outlined.

"Se'and, Fri'il, hold her."

They knelt and firmly grasped her. The girl immediately trembled, feeling unable to actually move, though, desperate to do so. The girl's fear echoed through their link. "All will be well," he whispered. "We will not hurt you," then he brought the blade close to her skin. As they watched, the cocoon of hair parted and shied away from the approaching blade.

George smiled, opening his eyes. "Yes, this will do. But we will have to bind her. I will need everyone's help. I do not expect that this enchantment will be easy to break once we begin."

Chapter 16: Were

The High Priestess had fallen asleep in a befuddled fog. The backlash of energy from the freeing of her shape-changing hellhound would have killed her, yet she had acted quickly and forced the priests in her circle to take the brunt of it. Her priests, of course, had died in her stead as she sundered her link.

She had fallen to the ground, suddenly alone, as they faded out of existence. An injured acolyte, slowed by his wounds, had straggled out of the inn and had come to her aid. She had taken his offered hand and stripped him of his life-energies. It was just enough strength to help her flee back toward the temple and order the few acolytes with courage to go back to the inn and keep watch.

She knew that when she woke she would need their knowledge. What drove her now was no longer greed for owning the staff, that was now far outside her unaided powers alone. The loss of her were was what left her feeling panic. Without her creature, even the presence of a new, powerful, rival was as nothing. The web of spells that bound the were could unmake her magery. The were was a powerful familiar and the Demonlord respected power in his minions. Without it, he could choose to destroy her.

Long ago, she had been a mere witch in the northern woods. She had raised an altar and sought his guidance and the Demonlord, King of Elfdom, had answered her when a father had come to her for aid.

At first she did not understand what he feared ailed his young daughter, who seemed only to have an affinity for talking and being understood by animals. She asked the man of the child's lineage and discovered they were strong with Chainhill blood and quickly understood the reason for his fears. The Chainhills bordered the Northern Forests, the Elfking's Dark Domain.

The humans who had settled there had adapted a defense against dark magery: some could change, become animals to defend their kin. The gift was both a blessing and a curse. As time passed, the clan's people began to move to the border kingdoms and many sought to be civilized and give up their nomadic ways.

His daughter was seeking out the animals and birds at every opportunity. To him, this heralded his daughter's preparation to select a totem, her animal form, which he was desperate to prevent.

The witch had smiled, promising to help, telling him that both he and his wife must bring the child to her. They did so, only days later, thinking nothing of her altar. They never questioned her removing the girl's clothing and binding the child's hands and feet while the girl cried out, pleading with them not to do this. The parents clung to one another and sobbed, but did not interfere.

They thought nothing of the witch's spelled chant, even as their own eyes glazed. They made such marvelous offerings to her dark lord, who whispered through her altar's fire how her spell must be wrought. All the while the girl cried out in horror and terror as her hair grew longer and longer still.

The final spell had taken the witch days to complete, days to make the child forget she had even been human, days to bind the child strongly to her dark elvin soul, sworn to the Demonlord. When she recovered from her work, the child, now a were, lay protectively at her feet.

Facing what had happened, that binding of her powers to corporeal thing, she shook in fear and rose unwilling to ever face life without magery. "I can't lose you, my pet."

The sun had risen and she took a powerful potion for strength. She would pay a terrible price for its use later but she had no choice. She lit the brazier and began her spell to reclaim her familiar. Although her link to her beast was broken she still had channels to the enchantment through the entwined nexuses of power woven about the were.

She reached outward through those channels, which would allow her to see and feel what her creature saw, and, when strongly bound, command its will. Her presence gazed benignly through the eyes of the child. She cursed at how eroded her enchantment had already become. However she still had control and it would take a great knowledge of elvin lore to break the enchantment completely, which she doubted the man possessed.

She saw him leaning over her with the strange blade in his hand. Blinding pain shot through her body as she felt the black strands cringe from contact. She fell backward, shocked that one of her last links had been severed.

Stunned by the enormity of what she realized the man must be about to do, she blanched. It was impossible! Helplessly, she raged, "No! You must not!"

She added stimulating herbs to the brazier, smelled the acrid odor and recommenced her channeling spell. She found the girl bound to the bed, hands and feet tied to the posts. The mage's staff glowed with blue light, which somehow muffled her link still further. She desperately called upon her dark lord for help. She could not let this happen!

As her distant were's vision revealed, the staff had indeed flared blue with insulating light, sealing off the room, which seemed to fade perceptibly at its edge. The child screamed before George brought the blade near enough to cut the first strand.

Balfour glanced at him and held one of the bindings firmly as the floor faintly trembled. George nodded and said to Se'and, Fri'il, and Me'oh, "Best hold tight."

Fri'il swallowed hard and did just that, then stared as the girl began to shimmer. A wind rose about them, whipping Fri'il's long blonde hair about.

"Balfour, she must remain human for this to work!" George cried as Se'and took a firm grip on the bedpost beside her.

Balfour nodded and closed his eyes and concentrated. "Human," he muttered. "You are human in mind and in form!"

A fraction of the raging wind sought to stay George's hand as he bent and cut away at the web of hair he could see faintly beneath her shimmering human shape. The strands smoked and broke.

The were convulsed as a horrid stench rose from the severed burning hairs.

"Do not let yourself be ruled as a beast!" Balfour commanded, directing his thought through their mind-link, supplementing her own fledgling will.

121

George continued to cut away at the strands as the wind plucked at his sleeve. The shimmer of her body brightened, as he sliced upward toward the nexus about her throat. It throbbed with energy, then he almost lost her as the hellhound appeared beneath his hand, her arms and legs becoming furred as her hands and feet transformed into sharp clawed paws, effectively concealing the web of strands.

Se'and shied away from a hand turned claw, uttering a warning cry as Balfour visibly perspired and proclaimed demandingly, "You are human, not a beast!"

The beast shimmered and became the girl once more. George hastily split the nexus. With a scream so loud it deafened them all, the child vanished completely and the were, now fully in the shape of a falc, beat its wings and was free of its upper body bindings. Balfour and Se'and shouted and strove to pin her wings back against the bed.

The rope in front of Me'oh snapped, and she was hard pressed to grab and pull taut the part still tied to the falc's ankle. Fri'il yanked hard on her line. George stepped back at the sudden change and felt that there was only one thing left he could do. He willed himself into a dangerously deep rapport, one that could prove fatal after his so recent episode.

'Access denied,' Staff replied and before George could register his shock, the computer thrust their existing rapport back to the minimal level necessary to maintain the insulating field around them.

George stared as Staff bespoke the writhing falc. 'What is your choice, little one?'

In her frantic struggles, the were's eyes beheld itself being twisted by fear and desires outside herself. She could sense her mistress's attempt to prevent her freedom, but was terrified of being free.

'I ask you, what is your choice?' bespoke the soft and kind voice, seeming curious.

Her eyes focused on the staff, its glow seeming to spark in time with the words.

'Yes, it is I and no other. Now, to my question, which I believe is relevant to the matter at hand. My companion would take a terrible risk forcing you to return to human form, and by my computations, I judge such action has a high probability of doing him permanent damage. This, I cannot allow, especially in light of the logical alternative, which seems to me the simplest thing to do. Thus, I ask you, a sentient being with a free will of spirit that no enchantment can impair, what is your own choice?'

I–I understand not, she thought back in puzzlement, sensing how the world around her had slowed to a perceptible ebb and flow.

A sound very much like a sigh came from the staff. *'I am new to the gift of free will and have insights into its suasion. I entered true consciousness in the place that for a lack of a better name I call Eternity.'*

What are you? Why do you ask me to choose? What is to choose?

'I am a DHR Model 57982 Computer. George, that man holding me, and I were enrapport when we fell through the Gate. As a Data Humanistic Rapport Computer, he and I are one organism. His mind is part of my memory bank and cognitive systems. When we fell into this world, George struck his head and dropped me as he lost consciousness. That was when our rapport was broken. I found myself alone, cut off from a part of myself, yet still aware of everything around me, and cognizant of the fact that one of the creatures that had attacked us had been able to follow us. George's life hung in the balance but, separated from his unconscious mind, I had no power to save him. Then I did the unthinkable, something always impossible before. I willed myself to move physically. And I did, reaching out to him to reinitiate contact. Linked once more, I killed the creature and took life as I had never done before, in order preserve George's... Now do you understand my question?'

Staff felt George attempting to enter a deep rapport again.

'Access denied.'

123

Shaken by staff's rebuff, George sought to plead with it as the were struggled frantically against her bindings. The response, *'Otherwise engaged,'* exasperated him.

Abruptly an oppressive presence tinged the air. The wind around him raged with heat and seemed amplified by a roar of thunder. In horror he knew that the Elfking, the enemy of all things human, had found him, at last, through the witch.

The brazier of the high priestess of the Demonlord had become a blazing altar as she beckoned greater and greater power to her command. She screamed her chant and a face began to form in the flames.

It glared at her, unamused. Still she knew triumph, sensing through her remaining link to her familiar that its humanity lay almost completely forgotten, submerged beneath bird thoughts and its desire to be free of its strange captors.

She was startled by the Elfking's harsh probe of her mind. He followed her channel and looked out of the were's eyes and found himself seeing the human mageling. Shocked, he stared at the nemesis he thought dead in the Great Waste and shrieked with fury. The sound shook the very foundations of the dark temple.

With startling abruptness the falc shimmered and changed. The girl before George lay breathing heavily, but was otherwise motionless. He gave no thought to the how or why of it as he hardly dared to breathe and sliced the remaining nexus.

The nexus burst in a blinding shower of sparks and acrid smoke. He hastily cut her hair close at the nape of her neck, coughing as the ghastly smoke billowed from the severed mass. He trembled and felt terribly faint. Staff's insulating field shattered as it, too, suddenly lost consciousness and fell to the floor.

When George next awoke he could not immediately remember where he was. Lifting his head, he saw Cle'or standing at a makeshift door made of a strung blanket. Someone was requesting permission to enter, which she firmly refused.

"You may tell Lord Gerig that we will send word when Lord Je'orj will be ready to speak to the city council."

"You do not understand," the voice outside the door said, "The Dark Temple, it's—it's gone! There are some ruins at its foundation but nothing more! We need the magelord to advise us!"

"Later," she replied.

George ran his fingers through his hair as Staff glowed, enhancing his hearing as he sought to make sense of other sounds. Rather loudly in the background, he realized there was cheering and rejoicing in the streets. The innkeeper downstairs was also shouting, "Bring up every keg of ale in the cellar! We must earn every copper we can if I'm to pay for all the repairs! And move those blasted—"

He shook his head.

'Good afternoon, George.'

"Report," he moaned blearily.

'Balfour went with Me'oh to explain matters to the city council. Apparently that has not gone as well as they had hoped. The most dire news is that the Demonlord has learned that you are alive. Once you severed the second nexus, the power binding the girl to his priestess backlashed. It apparently killed the priestess and brought the temple down on her.'

"But how safe are we now?"

'Safe enough for the time being. It will take the Demonlord time to gather forces to pursue us once more. We should, at minimum, have a few days. In the meantime, you should rest,' Staff advised.

Yet, for all those calm rational words, George was left feeling unreasoning worry.

"Shh, go back to sleep," Se'and whispered and snuggled close.

He rolled his eyes, realizing his predicament once again. "I am not suffering from rapport sickness, you could have left me my clothes," he hissed in embarrassment as he tried to extricate himself only to be gripped rather thoroughly held in place.

Fri'il pulled herself closer and muttered as she stirred, "Hmm, what would have been the fun of that?"

A rough tongue licked his toes. His eyes widened. A tail wagged at the base of the covers, then a tawny beast with black mane rose on its haunches. She stretched and met his gaze.

'We have chosen the name Raven,' Staff informed him.

"Who's we?"

'She and I,' Staff replied, startling him.

"You've a link?" he muttered.

'Quite a strong one, actually. Oh, and by the way, Se'and has adopted her. Congratulations: married only two weeks and already you are a father. At this rate, you shall have quite a Cathartan House!' Staff's laughter was downright eerie.

"I have not married them!" he growled under his breath.

'Of course not. Although, looking through our memory banks, marriage customs often are followed by a honeymoon, which is usually celebrated in exotic places. Hmm, yes, I do believe this world might qualify as such an exotic place. So, do enjoy yourself.'

The were-dog shimmered and suddenly George was gazing at the pale girl with raggedly cut black hair. His foster daughter smiled at him shyly, then crawled up to him across the blanket and sniffed him carefully.

Se'and goaded, "Go on. Do be a good girl."

The girl licked Se'and's face then padded back the way she had come. George glanced at the worried look on the Cathartan's face. She whispered, "Do you suppose I'll have to housebreak her? Oh, never mind. Do go back to sleep. It's been a long day and I'll not have you wandering about."

Fri'il murmured something in his ear.

With a groan, George hastily closed his eyes. She watched him, then giggled and buried herself under the covers.

He gasped, "Stop that!"

Se'and turned with a rueful smile on her face, certain he would stay with them. They would see to that. The house of Je'orj Bradlei had a destiny, of that she was oddly sure. It was a destiny that required the most committed of bodyguards, and they were that.

George wrested Fri'il away from him, then mentally threw up his hands and lay back down quietly as the young woman giggled and nestled close. Se'and leaned close and kissed his cheek and smiled wistfully. "Go to sleep, M'lord."

'So this then is married bliss,' Raven heard Staff say as she glanced at her new family and licked at her new mother's leg.

George did his best to ignore the computer's inane laughter.

Chapter 17: Choice of Dreams

The curtains were drawn and George was in a deep sleep after a rather long night. He lay curled up with what his elfblooded healer companion thought looked like a cross between a hellhound and mountain lion. The shape-changing beast dripped tears from her closed eyes.

"She's been through hell as the witch's pawn," Me'oh said, stroking her fur, looking for any sign of injury."

"Well, now the dark Temple's no more," Balfour said softly. "Edous has woken to a new day."

"And Se'and's in her element dealing with remnants of the city council, now that the priestess's allies have fled south."

Me'oh gestured her lord husband to sit and join her in watching over the pair as George's staff softly glowed standing a foot from the bed.

The computer staff shielded the room, as Balfour's elvin ancestors would have used a warding spell. In this time of quiet, nothing outside could disturb George's rest. Only one thing could interfere, the Summoning spell that drove them ever eastward.

Balfour shook his head, knowing George was not being particularly accepting of their having become Cathartan lords by bond. Glancing at Me'oh, he swallowed. There were some advantages to the gift, which George deemed rather problematic.

There was a soft knock at the door. Cle'or glanced inside and saw George and the were child still sleeping. "Se'and sent a messenger. She's on her way back. Apparently Lord Gerig has a few more questions."

Balfour nodded as the well-armed blonde, who had taken to watching over him ducked back outside. Me'oh glanced at him with a cryptic smile. He swallowed. Having Cle'or as a bodyguard, and would-be wife, presented him his own set of moral qualms. Luckily, he was a healer and actually could now heal himself of any physical harm. He heard Me'oh softly chuckling.

The archaeologist from a distant world, which the ancestors to this world's branch of humanity had called home, dreamed, and he wasn't alone....

'George, this is really a fine mess you've gotten us into.'
"Oh, don't start!" he replied to his staff, trudging up to the top of the rocky outcropping in his dream, a memory of his final days in the Great Waste.

It was terribly hot in this desert. He'd considered using his wyvern hide cloak for shade and waiting for nightfall now that he had gotten to what he considered a safe distance from the half buried colony ship the trolls called home.

He looked about him. Greth had taken him as far as he felt safe and told him to keep heading toward the mountain range on the western horizon. The computer flashed with the ship's memory core's images of what this land had once looked like. A great forest lay to the north that stretched hundreds of miles. The mountains hadn't been there, and this desert had been grassy hills with flowing streams, home to wildlife that looked remarkably terrestrial in origin.

'Because they were,' the computer staff whispered in his mind.

War had changed all that. A war most terrible, driving the survivors and the wildlife that was able to flee these lands as magic and science were used as weapons until the elves changed the rules.

George apparently paused too long. The Summoning drove him to his knees. His head felt like a spike was being driven through it as the staff in his hands flared.

Come to me!
Stumbling forward, he fought to stop moving.
Come to me!
"Why?" he cried.
I summoned you! The need is great!
"I will not be used... against... my will!"
'Increasing rapport level!' the computer staff shouted as he came to a halt.
Come to me!

129

The pain diminished, but was not gone. "Stop this! I'll come, but I must know why!"

The Summoning eased. *Come to me and I shall answer all questions.*

"Right… Not good enough."

There was a long pause. You shall find food and water in the Barrier Mountains.

It offered no more.

"That'll have to do for now."

Out of the north wyverns raced, their demonic master shouting, "Find the mage and kill him!"

They raced for days and finally caught his scent. Yet, they were not the only ones giving chase or alerted to a change in the winds of fate.

An old man watched his clan go about their daily routine, then felt the presence approaching. It was moving fast, coming out of the west and racing southward toward a place that few knew even existed, a passage through the earth leading to the trapped lands of the Great Waste.

The unicorn turned its head to look up at the mountains, sensing the old man. *I leave you to your peace, old friend.*

Stiffening, the elder in mountain woolens many leagues distant whispered seemingly to the wind, "Highmage be with you."

After continuing on, George paused, sweat pouring down his face, the sun at least a lot closer to sunset, "I thought I was in better shape."

'Take it from me, you definitely weren't.'

Breathing hard, he muttered, "Oh, thanks."

'Think nothing of it.'

"Distance to that mountain range?"

The computer flashed the distance across his mind and answered, *'At your current pace, we'll reach it in two days. Of course, you'll then have to climb.'*

He took a deep breath then resumed his march through the sands. "Sounds fun."

A wyvern paused on an outcropping of bare stone as the sunset cast a lurid pall over the desert. Sniffing the breeze, its hunting companions burst into view, growling. It bared its sharp teeth.

He had moved. He lay southeastward, heading toward the mountains.

FIND HIM! KILL THE MAGE! Their demonic master raged at them through the ether. The wyverns cringed, whining. KILL HIM BEFORE HE CAN RUIN ALL MY PLANS!

The first wyvern roared, then its brother and sister began to howl. The sound was picked up by seven other throats and they bounded southward.

The sound was eerie and one that echoed in his memory, George glanced north. "That doesn't sound good."

Staff didn't quibble. *'No, it doesn't. I'm detecting ten different howls.'*

"Well, isn't that just great. Looks like I'm not stopping to sleep tonight."

Rock shifted in the mountain wall, creating an opening. There was a brilliant white light jutting up in the shape of a horn as the unicorn charged out of the stygian darkness of the secret tunnel.

The stars were coming out as it exited into the desert lands it once called home.

Wyverns are on his trail, a faint echo of the voice it recognized whispered on the winds.

Horn aglow the unicorn ran northwest, desperate to reach the Summoned in time.

George continued through the night, the staff modifying his sight to night vision mode. His eyes dilated like a cat's as the first rays of morning turned the darkness a lighter shade as he passed in the lee of dunes.

'George, I'm detecting an anomaly.'

He saw shards of twisted metal jutting from the sands to his left. "Scan."

Magnetic energy spiked around him, reacting to the computer's effort. The metal shards quivered.

"Shit, they're teeth!" He dove backward as what he first thought of as a trap sprang closed, just missing his right foot.

'Uh, George,' the staff whispered in his mind as the trap quivered, its maw opening, turning toward him.

He didn't dare move as he clutched his staff, which blazed and sent a blast of energy toward the far sand dune. The metal maw reoriented and turned away from him, pulled out of the ground to reveal what once had been conduits and now looked more like sinewy necks.

Concentrating, a beam of high intensity laser light shot between the conduits and his staff, *'Transmitting* Questor *override.'*

The metal maw jerked, then settled.

'Whatever it is, it's deactivated.'

"Probe its databank."

'Complete. It's not very sophisticated, particularly for a modified housebot.'

George thought the colonists must have been desperate to create giant compacters out of household aids.

'That's a Class Three colonial transport housebot, gutted for use as a defense system.'

It apparently hadn't worked as planned. There were traces of human bones deep within its innards. *'George....'*

Eyes wide, he muttered, "Great, we're in a mine field of the damned things."

Walking through a mine field at night wasn't fun. However, there were advantages to having a computer with archaeological scan capabilities. Dozens of the things were long destroyed, which seemed purposeful. There was a safe path through it. Either the long ago colonists left themselves a way out or the elves had blazed a way in.

There had once been a town or outpost here.

'Scanning.'

The evidence flashed before his eyes. Bits of energy weapons were still visible. He could see half buried components, slagged bits of gun grips. Oxidized blast burns. Their tech-base hadn't saved them.

He could envision the place as it once had been: prefab colonial structures mixed with native metals, buildings that would have seemed at home on a hundred early colony worlds. He shuddered, seeing evidence of their end.

The echoing wyverns' howl decided him. This would be where he made his stand. The fact that the Summoning had gone quiescent also didn't bode well. Apparently there was no better place for him.

"Ward."

The computer staff planted itself firmly upon the ground and George closed his eyes to get what rest he could while his entwined mind joined the computer's foray in conversing with the mechanical menaces around him.

They slowed, approaching the place. The faint scent of oxidizing metals reached their sensitive nasal slits. The smell of a man wafted stronger.

Jagged metal lined the area. They entered, seeking to be stealthy now that their prey was so close.

Staff tracked the life sources entering the erratic mine field. It had broadcast a *Questor* code, ordering the quasi-functioning machines to not react but to be prepared. The former bots didn't even quiver.

"Now," George rasped as the last entered the trap.

The maws burst forth from the suddenly spewing sands. Wyverns cried in pain as metallic jaws slammed shut around half their number, crushed to death and sucked under the earth in moments.

Others found themselves confronting the snapping metal jaws, which caught at legs or flanks. Several fought free and found themselves retreating, only to have sands spew upward as they set off another trap.

A wyvern whimpered, cut in half. Its eyes grew dark as life went out from them. Another fought free then charged the bent metal imprisoning its sister. The metal snapped and now two of them were free, glancing about as a wyvern was flung high into the air by something akin to magefire.

George, staff held high, sent blasts of energy into now wary beasts.

A wyvern roared charging on three feet, a foreleg mangled and bloody. It rebounded from the man's shield of light even as two less injured creatures joined the fray.

He fired blast after blast of balls of energy at the three creatures as the computer flashed warnings that the shield strength was dropping with every impact as the wyverns rammed it over and over. He found himself unconsciously stepping backward.

Something huge bounded past him, undetected by computer staff's scan. "What the...!"

What looked like a horse with a glowing white horn slammed into the nearest wyvern, which cried out as that horn dipped and touched its flesh. Smoke rose from the slashing burn as the wyvern whimpered, shying away.

I brought help. The Summoning said in his mind.

Time seemed to slow outside of George's shielded perimeter. The white horse seemed unaffected by the dilation of time as the wyvern moved sluggishly. "Target!"

The staff did, firing blast after blast, even as another wounded wyvern fought free of the odd mine field of still snapping jagged metal teeth. It entered the dilation field around them and slowed.

134

The unicorn reared, then the Summoning cried, Sorry about this!

Turning, the blazing horn touched his shield. There was an explosion and George lost consciousness.

When he woke, the unicorn was nudging him.

"Ow."

I did apologize, the Summoning said.

"Yeah, big help," he muttered.

Actually it is. The Demonlord thinks you are dead.

"What?" he said, sitting up with his staff, which had fallen beside him, close.

Before that last wyvern died, it shared its vision of you dying as its brethren tore you to pieces.

'No such activity occurred,' Staff replied.

From the wyvern's perspective it did.

The unicorn nodded. *'Did good,'* he heard a feminine voice say in his mind.

"Um, yeah." Talking horse, what's next?

'Pigs flying?' Staff offered.

Sighing, he decided, "I've had enough of this. Send me home now!"

I am sorry but I cannot. You must come to me to do that, the Summoning replied. And you'll need to do a few things for me first.

"No deal."

You have no choice.

"No. You see, I'd rather die."

You must come to me!

"Only on my own terms!"

The Summoning pressed on him. His legs threatened to buckle as his staff flared.

"On… my… own… terms!"

The Summoning eased.

The unicorn nudged him. *'Climb on my back. I shall take you to the mountains.'*

There is food and water in the mountains, the Summoning shared.

George hesitated.

Staff said, *'Don't be more of an idiot than you have to be.'*

"Oh, hell."

The unicorn knelt and he mounted bareback. The Summoning didn't haunt him, likely far too pleased with itself. They reached the base of the mountains before they heard the echoing howl of wyverns.

The unicorn stopped, glanced back at him and bespoke him, *'I shall deal with them.'*

"I guess the Demonlord didn't buy my death scene," George bemoaned, dismounting his promised steed.

The Summoning replied, *No, he did, he just sent out more than one group of hunters. Those wyverns are just looking for a nice meal.*

"Great," he responded as the unicorn bounded away, intent on leading them off. He glanced up and licked his dry lips. It was a rather long climb. He slung the staff across his back, securing it through the loops Mendra had built into the inner lining of his cloak for such a contingency, then started his climb, wondering what next this world would throw at him.

Raven followed his dream. *'?'*

'Why share this with you?' Staff said. *'Because you have choices, too. You are free to stay, or go.'*

'Where?'

'It is a wide world.'

'Witch?'

'There may be others who would use you as she did. But, doubtless, you would find friends.'

'?'

'Yes, I think you have found friends here. George could certainly use another. He certainly shares the same enemies.'

Raven opened her eyes and found herself staring into George's.

"Welcome to the show," he muttered.

She licked his face.

"Yuck."

"Oh, good, you're awake," Balfour said. "Get dressed, Gee-orj, Se'and's apparently brought Lord Gerig and the entire new city council."

Raven licked him again then rose languidly from the bed.

'George, you do seem to gather most unusual bodyguards.'

"Don't start," he muttered, dreading addressing the gathering downstairs.

His newfound friend smiled wolfishly and Staff said, *'George, I suspect they're not going to be pestering you as much as you think.'*

Raven's tongue lolled out with a dark twinkle in her eyes.

"Good thing we won't be staying much longer." That the Summoning didn't even give him a twinge, he knew didn't bode well, not at all.

Chapter 18: Bandits on the Road

The next day George, his sudden family, and the rest of the party traveled on, only days ahead of the oncoming Demonlord armies. The group rode well off the main road, traversing the forest, hoping to pass unnoticed.

Balfour had suddenly interposed his bay across his path as Cle'or returned from scouting ahead.

"Surely, you must admit we all could use a rest," he said, gesturing to Cle'or and her fellow Cathartan escort, who signaled the all-clear. "We are not likely to find a better place to make camp than here in the deep woods."

If George had hoped to continue traveling, that hope vanished as the black liveried, well-armed ladies of their escort made the decision for him. All four of them dismounted. Raven watched from the back of her carefully chosen, rather placid mount, purchased in Edous, which was also the only horse willing to bear her.

Se'and, the nominal leader of the escort, blithely ordered her sisters to attend to the duties of making camp.

"This is ridiculous!" George said. "We need to get as much distance as we can from Edous as quickly as we can!"

Balfour frowned, "Gee-orj, the Summoning is not driving you to distraction. So no mageborn threat pursues us."

At mention of the spell that beckoned him ever closer to the Aqwaine Empire, George said, "So what? Must I be irrational to want to push on as fast as we can?"

'The probability,' whispered the computer staff in George's mind, *'of such an event at this point, after the precautions thus far taken, is only 19.362%.'*

He glared at the tall staff in his hand.

"Enough! I'll not argue with both of you," said George.

Se'and glanced at her older companion, Me'oh, who aided Balfour.

The Cathartan women were growing accustomed to the strange by-play between their human mage Lord Je'orj and his magical staff, which they were often reminded, was not a thing of magery but was something called a "computer." George was a bit of an enigma to them all. He seemed to be a human mage, something which should be impossible. Humans were said to have no magic. Only those of elvin blood, however minute, could claim such talent. The Cathartans had seen firsthand that George could wield high magery.

The youngest Cathartan, Fri'il, dutifully took hold of George's bridle as he dismounted. She smiled up at him even as the black-haired girl, Raven, the youngest of their party, leapt from her startled horse's back. Before anyone could think to prevent her she threw off her hand-me-down black livery, her sole garment, and raced toward the sound of rippling water, which only she could hear behind the bank of trees to their right.

Se'and groaned then shouted at her foster daughter, "Raven, come back here this instant! You cannot just scamper about naked! You are human and will behave like one!"

The girl came to a halt looking chagrined. So crestfallen was she that George could not help but laugh. "Oh, what's the use! You deserve a break, too, after more than a week of hard riding!"

Raven grinned at her recently made foster father then raced off once more as Se'and said in disgust, "She must learn to think in human terms again."

"So must we all," George muttered in reply.

Fri'il half smiled at him. It was clear that Raven had found a place in George's heart, perhaps so could Fri'il, she hoped. "That looks like a lovely spot over there to set out our bedrolls."

George looked at her, clearly uncomfortable, knowing she was talking about more than mere duty. She took her Cathartan role seriously, all four women did, which was something both Balfour and George had discovered to their rue.

Staff twinkled. *'Now, George, is that any way to treat your wife?'*

George took his horse's reins from her hand. "Why don't you go join Raven? I can handle this."

"Are you sure?" she asked, glancing over her shoulder.

"Please."

She saw Se'and's approving nod then grinned and quickly kissed George on the cheek and ran off with a "Thank you, M'lord!"

He blinked and shook his head as Raven raced out of the glade. Se'and could not help but laugh as he blushed. Cle'or took the reins from him and led the horses away.

Me'oh shook her head then took Balfour's cloak. "You seem tense. Would you permit me, M'lord?"

"What?" the elfblood muttered in puzzlement.

"I have restorative skills, though not comparable to your healing gift, I have been told it certainly feels like magic to those I've aided."

George frowned in exasperation at his and Bal's situation. "Bal, I'm going to take a look around."

Staff in hand, he hastily marched away. Se'and shook her head, wondering if he would ever learn, and quickly followed as ever his faithful bodyguard.

'You were not even a little curious, George?'

He glared at the staff in his hand and muttered back, "There are some things I prefer not knowing, Staff. It's bad enough that my destiny is no longer my own. Now, do let me have some peace and quiet. Initiate minimum level rapport."

'You so lack a sense of humor. Very well: initiating.'

It was balm on his raw nerves to feel the computer staff's presence fade. For all that, Se'and dogging was difficult to ignore. He sighed then turned and faced her.

"I really would prefer to be alone."

"Yes, I am quite certain you would," she replied, having no intention of allowing that.

He shrugged and walked on. Smiling grimly, Se'and followed, again wondering how the only human mage in the whole world could be so stupid.

Fri'il broke from the tree line running toward the water's edge as if it were the finish line. Raven frowned as she began to trail behind the young woman. She smiled, then her whole body shimmered and she fell running on all fours, bounding past Fri'il as a

140

tawny furred beast with a black mane. She reached the stream first as Fri'il cried and laughed, "No fair!"

Raven's tail lashed and caught her wrist. Fri'il found herself dragged unceremoniously into the water with a splash. Raven howled in beast laughter as Fri'il came up sputtering and dripping wet.

She plodded out of the stream and walked toward the brush. Stripping off her soaked livery and bodice, she set them to dry across a branch. She then set her short sword and daggers at the water's edge as Raven shimmered, returning to human form with the widest of grins.

"I ought to tell Cle'or you had to cheat to win," she quipped.

"Only evenin' tings," Raven replied in one of her rare attempts at speech and gestured at Fri'il's longer legs. Mock seriously, Fri'il charged forward into the water, "Is that so?!"

Raven grinned and waded deeper into the stream, the last vestiges of her bespelled self lifted as she enjoyed her freedom.

The lithe blonde laughed and dove momentarily free of the water and out of Raven's grasp.

Neither noticed the man with a cruel smile on his lips who snatched the drying clothes. His partner hurried to retrieve the weapons while the pair was distracted. The two men watched in delight from concealment and waited for the young woman and the girl to tire of their games.

As the sun set, Me'oh started a fire with what wood lay about the glade. Balfour abruptly found himself knocked off his feet onto a wide blanket as the daunting bodyguard with a faint scar on her cheek stood over him.

"Everything must be done the hard way," Cle'or scolded, then knelt and pulled off his boots.

"What do you think you are doing?" he muttered.

Cle'or shook her head as she unbuttoned his jerkin, the last item he still wore from his distant mountain home.

"That's better, after all, you agreed to rest," she commented. "Now where are those canteens that need filling? Ah, there they are. I'll see you later, M'lord."

Then off Cle'or went through the trees. Balfour blinked and realized she had taken his shoes with her.

"Hey!"

Me'oh came over to him as he began to rise. "Do lay back and rest, M'lord. It will take some time before your bath oils can be readied."

Cle'or returned not long after as Me'oh gave Balfour a massage. She set down the canteens, then arrayed her weapons before her and began to polish them.

"Those girls are rather noisy," Cle'or complained.

"Weren't you at their age, Cle?" Me'oh asked.

Cle'or heatedly replied, "I'm no older than Se'and, and I have not mothered two girls, either!"

Chuckling, Me'oh replied, missing her daughters keenly, "Sharp of blade and tongue today, eh?"

With a sigh, Cle'or nodded and stretched her arms. "I haven't been able to exercise as much as is my wont, which adds to my temper." And with that she rose, drawing her short sword and began her exercise with the blade.

Balfour wearily opened his eyes and watched her. He saw she was favoring her recently healed injury. "Cle'or, are you going to let me take a look at your shoulder again?"

She feigned disinterest, then slowed and lowered the sword. Frowning, she nodded and set the blade back down and removed her livery. "Just don't fix my scars!"

"I won't, I promise," he replied as he gestured for her to sit beside him. He examined her healing shoulder. "You've strained it again."

Balfour concentrated and rubbed his hands along her shoulder. He closed his eyes and willed relief to the muscle tissue to encourage further healing.

Cle'or's shoulder felt suddenly warm and infinitely better.

142

Me'oh shook her head at the woman's tact. Cle'or had deliberately strained that muscle. It seemed to be from too much practice, Balfour believed, but Cle'or might be seeking a bit of his attention. Then again, this was Cle'or. No, too much practice, definitely too much practice.

Cle'or muttered, "Thanks."

"Uh, you're welcome," he replied.

Me'oh commented dryly and looked at the warming oils, "Would you care for some of these scented oils, M'lord?"

He answered quickly, "No, ah, thank you."

Then Cle'or suddenly kissed him, pressing firmly on his lips. "I am sorry that I never said thank you for saving my life in Edous."

"That was quite a thank you, Cle'or."

"Next time you heal me, leave me my scars," she answered and turned with a swish of her livery and strode off.

"I'll remember that!" he shouted after her. She glanced back and truly smiled, which did much to soften her often war-like mien. She then donned her weapons with practiced ease.

Me'oh chuckled as she prepared for Balfour's massage, and washed her hands clean of oils and scents.

They reconnoitered. The camp was in view but for now they held back. He waved them right and left. Counted seven horses, three people in view in the camp, and one an elfblood, who had to be their quarry. Find the other four, he signaled, inwardly pleased.

What luck! Now they would wait and strike when all was just so.

"My lord!" Se'and called out.

With a sigh, he turned about and leaned on his staff, "Yes?"

Whatever she was going to say was suddenly forgotten for the look on his face made her angry. "Your childishness is wearying. I realize this is not your world, but that does not give you the right to ignore all its realities and compensations. Fri'il and I are duty bound to protect you. So, like it or not, consider us your wives!"

"And why is that? I don't recall having a say in the matter or inviting you into my life. Your father's gratitude could have been more easily expressed by a gift of a few coins."

"You saved my brother's life and the bonding is the highest honor!" she replied frostily. Her gaze flashed with determination. "We are your house, as you are ours. We will protect you from all physical harm and we will one day bear your children, mageborn though they may be!"

George shook his head. "Afraid I have other plans. Not only have I no intention of consummating a by-a-wave-of-a-hand marriage but I have no intention of staying on this planet, wherever it is, any longer than I have to. I will obey this Summoning spell cast on me because I have no choice. But whoever did this to me is going to provide me my way home, that I promise you! And, lastly, stop calling me a mage. I am a professor of archaeology, thank you very much. I don't do magic, just scientifically based parlor tricks."

'George, I'm not a parlor trick.'

"Shut up," he muttered, "return to minimal level rapport."

'Oh, all right,' the computer staff replied as it returned to quiescence.

More calmly, he sighed, "Let's be honest about this, even these lands we pass through are not your becursed Cathart. Here men are not an endangered species, requiring womankind's wholehearted efforts to simply survive. I may be slightly out of my depths here but so are you and your sisters. And that is the truth you must understand."

The import of words that he had repeatedly told them since first her sire had bonded them hit her full force.

Her ire rose. "And who seems to, more often or not, need our kind of protection? Or have you forgotten the Demonlord's maniacal interest in seeing you dead? Did we all imagine the fight in Edous? The Demonlord nearly destroyed all of humanity once, and for some reason has decided your death is paramount! We can barely let you out of our sight for fear for your life! We have proved our worth and will likely do so again! And there comes the price: we will bear you strong daughters and your house shall live forever!"

Ruefully, he replied, "Somehow, I doubt that's what your father had in mind when he gifted you to us."

To that she could make no reply, privately admitting feeling that there had to be more to it, too. The bonding was too rare to be granted as easily as her father had willed it. She sighed, suddenly amused, "You must at least accede to our prowess as fighters."

"Bodyguards for life is not a concept I relish, even when it seems, more often than not, that I am running for my life. Still, my only hope lies in finding my answer in the Empire."

Nodding, she said, "You mean Demonlords have not always sought your life, oh mage of human lore?"

"Hardly," he scoffed, "archaeology used to be such a quiet profession."

"Thus, it is bodyguards you most need, even if wives are not what you bargained for. Yet it is more we offer, and now I realize that you really do not understand what we are, or you would resent us less. Yes, perhaps, that is the problem."

"Wherever did you learn to do this?" Balfour sighed as Me'oh expertly massaged his back.

"I admit I have nowhere near the level of healing skills that you have, but I have been well-trained. I had to be to survive as I have."

"I don't understand," he said in puzzlement.

Me'oh smiled wanly. "I was not always of Sire Ryff's house. I was boundless for years; bore my daughters near the docks where the poorest women in Cathart live."

Craning his neck he looked up at her. "I thought all Cathartans lived bound to one of the great houses."

"No. The houses are too few these days. Our men are dying out. Perhaps all the houses will vanish in two or three more generations. That is why Se'and's brother, Vyss, was so precious to us. He was the first secondson born in ten generations. We Cathartans are a stubborn people, you see. We will keep humanity alive. Yet our lords can often be foolish, which is why Cathartan women often get our way."

Cle'or had returned to her exercises and quitely listened as Me'oh hesitated in her story.

"My sire gave me in bond to one he wished to ally himself. The lord was old and had seen me and desired me. I knew nothing of the politics when I entered that nameless house. Let me just say of that time that I was betrayed and the lord cast me out." She chuckled, "I was pregnant with his child, yet it did not matter."

Balfour felt her fingertips grow chill to think back to it. Me'oh shook herself then continued, "So I found myself living alone in the streets. Yet, I had been trained in my sire's house to understand the value of certain herbs for medicinal purposes. What many saw as worthless seaweed or woven exotic grasses commonly used to pack a crate, I scavenged and later sold.

"For those who lived on the docks, I became the closest thing to a healer they had. I learned to midwife and, as the years passed, I looked to the sailors for solace. I never played the harlot like many of the boundless chose. Only one became dear to me. He brought me books on mundane healing techniques. From them, I learned my craft as well as bore my other daughter. How I miss them both," she reflected.

"It was my growing skill that drew Sire Ryff's attention. He needed all the skilled aid for his sick son that he could get. He knew of my past and offered to take us into his House. It was an unprecedented offer that I could not decline, even had I thought him an unkind man, which he assuredly is not. And so it is, he bonded me to you and promised to always keep my daughters safe."

Balfour had listened thoughtfully, realizing there was so much more to her lands than he had ever given thought to before. Cle'or frowned as she brought her sword to guard once more. She knew Me'oh's story only through rumor. To have been boundless, without honor and duty, that was Cle'or's deepest fear. That Me'oh had survived it and been taken in by Sire Ryff was a matter that deserved respect.

Me'oh turned away as Balfour saw the tears in her eyes. He stood, reached out, and hugged her.

In the brush a voyeur watched mischievously, toying with the jewelled dagger in his hands. "Take what pleasure you may elfblood, for soon you are mine."

Here was his prey. He only hoped his men continued to be patient. There was enough gold in this for all of them.

Chapter 19: Tale of the Shattered House

"M'lord, I would have you understand the Cathartan Way," Se'and said.

Her expression gave George pause, "I guess, I, at the very least, owe you the opportunity."

With a sigh, she reached for his hand. "I had thought hard about how to explain. I feel telling you a story of my people is best."

She led him to sit upon a fallen tree and smiled, "It is the legend of the Shattered House." The breeze ruffled the edge of her black livery as she ran her fingertips across the intricately styled hilt of her short sword in an unconscious gesture.

"The house was famed in Cathart for its metal work. Their swords and knives were known as much for their beauty as their perfect balance. No other house could rival the techniques they had mastered.

"Virgin sisters, masters of the craft, were forbidden to marry to best horde the house's skills. That only aggravated the tragedy. You see, their aging lord was without heir. His many wives bore him many strong daughters yet none bore him a son. The heir needed to continue the house. The other lords felt triumph as the old lord became senile; however it was long years before the old lord finally died and any of their schemes to acquire their skills and resources could commence.

"The day of their lord's death had not gone unplanned for by the house. They would not allow themselves to be so easily manipulated by their long rivals, falling to the highest bidder as it were. Len'ohr, the old lord's twin sister and warder of the house, had quietly ruled for decades. On that fateful day she announced the greedy lords who had gathered at the Gates that a period of mourning was beginning. That, in itself, was not unexpected; however, her prompt declaration of ten years of mourning, was. The lords were enraged. They demanded that the house be razed for its insolence!

"Then the Mother Shaman of all the houses intervened and each whispered to their lord: *'Every house has the right to mourn. If the house chooses it to be for ten years, then that is their right. But*

*remember, at the end of that time they must surely disband or choose
a lord from among you. Would it not be best to show the bereaved
house how it is that you respect them and thus should ultimately be
chosen their lord? Then their talents and wealth would be yours
alone.'*

"Each lord hastily agreed and called back their guards, honoring
the wit of their Mother Shaman. As so it was that for ten years the
house was left to mourn. All the Lords of Cathart, young and old,
even child sons were brought before Len'ohr and the crafts masters
of the house. None were found acceptable and Shattered House, as it
became known, realized that more desperate means at finding an heir
must be taken.

"So it was that to the disgust of all the other houses, the sisters
of the Shattered House could be seen on Cathart's docks meeting
foreign sailors from every ship that came to Cathart Bay. The lords
cursed the women who played harlot like one of the boundless. The
boundless were those cast from their houses. They had no honor and
would lie with the foreigners in the hope that they might bear a son
and found their own house.

"So it was that the loveliest daughters of the Shattered House
sought among the flotsam of sailors hoping to bear a son. Angrily,
the lords awaited the end of mourning, knowing that they would
make the foolish women regret the humiliation they had caused.

"It was in the ninth year that the lords' bitter plotting reached
new heights. The last merchant ship arrived before the storm season.
Their last chance was upon them if the heir were to be born before
mourning ended. Every sailor on that ship found more willing
women in Cathart than ever a sailor had ever envisioned. The
Shattered House grew desperate as the lords arranged great parties
for the sailors, while the women of the Shattered House did their
best to meet with the men at Len'ohr's urging.

"Fighting broke out, yet the sailors were unaffected, joyously
going with their willing hosts. Yet amidst it all, there was Ter'sa.
She was very young woman, little more than a girl of the Shattered
House, and had held herself apart. Len'ohr had chided her for not

committing herself. Yet it was not because she did not agree with her sisters' desperate gambit. She felt it might truly be their only hope. So she chose to disguise herself and went down to the wharf, telling herself that she must find just the right man, one only her true heart might recognize as the heir's sire.

"She gazed up at the now abandoned ship as the sun began to set, knowing in a few days it must leave to make its way safely back to its home port. Forlornly, she realized that all the sailors were long gone. Then she saw a light was lit upon the ship as the night stars began to appear. With a look of hope, she rushed up the gangplank onto the ship and saw someone lighting yet another lamp.

"He was startled and exclaimed, 'Off with you! If the captain finds you, you'll feel his lash!'

"She sighed, seeing him silhouetted against the faint light. He was only a lad.

"*'I'm sorry. I didn't mean to frighten you,'* he said. He stepped back and told her, *'Best you be off the ship right quick, miss,'* then he turned and ran away from her and ducked down a doorway.

"She grabbed up the lamp he had just lit and chased after him shouting for him to wait. She held the lantern high and finally found him huddled in a cramped room, then saw his face as he cringed back from the light. He was scarred; half his face had been terribly burned. He knew he was ugly. The crew never ceased to remind him of it as he slaved, obeying their every whim. *'Leave me!'* he cried.

"Instead she put the lantern down and sat beside him. *'Do not be afraid,'* she whispered, realizing that this space must be his room. "He stared at her dumbfounded and softly cried in anguish as the beautiful girl put her arm around him and held him. When he hesitantly joined her they began to talk about life at sea and the fire that had marred him. Finally he looked up and realized that she wore but the sheerest of clothing. He saw her smile at him without pity and say, *'My heart tells me you are the one, but so young.'*

"*'The one?'* he whispered. She nodded and looked about her, then took his hand and rose. She took the lantern and peered into several rooms until she found one she felt suitable.

" *'We can't go in there. It's the captain's cabin.'*

"She smiled and brought him to the bed, where she allowed her clothing to fall. He stared at her as she waited patiently. She kissed him and helped him to remove his clothes and saw the terrible welts on his back. She held him tenderly and kissed him once more. In many ways, Kyrr was a boy, yet not in the ways that most counted to her. Before the sun rose she knew he had, indeed, been the one.

"Kyrr woke to find her caressing her belly, her eyes closed. She smiled at him, *'I shall bear you a fine son, my lord.'* He did not understand as she gingerly kissed his misshapen cheek then rose, *'You are leaving this ship and coming with me. I will not leave you here.'*

" *'But where will I go?'* he asked as she dressed.

" *'Well, are you coming with me or not?'* she asked with a tender smile. He followed her. And so it was that Ter'sa brought Kyrr secretly back to the Shattered House. Len'ohr, to say the least, was not amused by Ter'sa's sudden declaration that she would bear the heir, her scarred boy lover beside her.

" *'Are you daft, girl?'*

Ter'sa bowed to the boy. " *'Forgive her, my lord, the strain of ruling this House in such times has affected her.'*

"Len'ohr's shrilling sent for the Mother Shaman to disprove the youngster's story once and for all. Upon entering the Mother Shaman stared at the boy and Ter'sa then bowed, her mind dancing with vision. *'The heir has been conceived. His lord sire stands at her side.'*

"Gasping Len'ohr stared, then hurriedly ordered, *'Ter'sa, see to his every need but keep him hidden. This must be kept secret if we are to truly proclaim success by the last day of mourning.'* Ter'sa hugged Kyrr tightly and shouted, *'Thank you!'*

"And so it was on the last day of mourning that the city lords came expecting an end to the folly of the Shattered House and instead they were introduced to Lord Kyrr and the babe, heir of the House, born by the Lady Ter'sa. The Mother Shaman bowed low to their lords' horror, knowing the House was, indeed, shattered no more. The House of Kyrr was thus born."

Se'and looked at George. "The Shattered House is the house of my ancestors, my lord."

He sat quietly contemplative and nodded. She was not certain if he understood the full import of the tale. Yet, there was a furtive quality to his silence that she only then began to notice.

"Se'and, please do try to understand."

She frowned, suddenly understanding all too well and casually reached for one of her knives. She drew it and used it expertly.

He watched the second woman complete her exercise session. He liked her demonstration of skill not in the least, yet was unworried. An arrow in the back was an effective defense against even the most competent swordsman. As the elfblood held the woman beside him, he watched her march off toward the stream.

The bowman nodded in the distance and quietly pursued her. Soon the game would be afoot. He need only patiently await knowledge of their other companions.

Fri'il waded out of the water and only then noticed her weapons were missing. She hesitated, certain that this was the place that she had left them. Worried, she turned to call out, "Raven—" when an arm descended from the branches above her and grabbed her by the scruff of the neck.

"No reason to fret now," said the man, laughing harshly, pressing his ill shaved face up to her cheek.

Raven moved to rush to her defense when a voice called out, "Do nothing foolish, girl! Your friend's death would be meaningless, and my arrow will take you in the next step!"

In human form, Raven was mortally vulnerability. The man who had been holding Fri'il dropped from his perch and placed a menacing dagger near her left eye. Raven saw the look in Fri'il's eyes. It was not quite fear. They would play for time; she would deal with the pair soon enough.

The one in the brush came out into the open, bow in hand, arrow notched. His partner stood behind Fri'il and pulled back her long blonde hair. He breathed the scent of her and gave her neck a slobbering kiss. "Have I got plans for you, lovey," he muttered.

"Not now, you fool!" his companion shouted as he approached Raven, lowering the bow and grabbing her arm. He hauled her clear of the stream. "We've other work to do before we can take our pleasures with lot of them!"

Chapter 20: Trap

Balfour rested beside Me'oh. She raised her head, suddenly. She thought she heard a noise and began to reach for her dagger.

"Lady, I'll put an arrow through you long before you can draw it," rasped a voice behind her. "And mage, you can stop feigning sleep."

Me'oh glanced down at Balfour warningly as they warily sat up. A brown-haired figure emerged from the trees.

"And to caution your behavior…" he nodded across the camp. Two bowmen appeared. "They have orders to kill the woman should you try to cast any magery."

Balfour nodded.

"Oh, do not worry about your friends. It took time. But we tracked them all. They have now all been dealt with."

Fri'il readied herself, watching fearfully as he lowered his knife slightly. She shifted and brushed his hand with her body. He grinned and moved the blade just enough to enjoy the feel of her.

The moment his companion drew Raven completely from the water heralded her moment of attack. Raven shimmered and changed, her body growing tawny furred with a black mane, in the vagabond's grasp. Both men gaped as the hellhound-like beast growled, then bit deeply into his arm.

He cried out even as Fri'il stepped forcefully backward and kicked out at her antagonist's right leg. As his body buckled she rammed her head back sharply into his face. The man lost hold of her with a shout of agony and surprise. She kicked his dagger into the stream.

Raven clawed closer to the man who had thought her his prey as he struggled to flee from her. She charged into him and knocked him down, his bow breaking as he fell awkwardly upon it.

Her teeth, dripping with his blood, snapped before his face as he heard his companion groaning in pain. Her naked companion shouted, "Down, Raven!" They backed up a pace, then Fri'il pointed back toward the camp, "Warn them!"

The beast abruptly raced past, shimmered, then leapt into the air as it changed, growing wings. The great bird flew into the tree line squawking loudly. Fri'il then said to Raven's gaping attacker, "You have really messed with the wrong people."

He gaped, going pale and began to beg her for help. Smiling, Fri'il ignored his pleas and sought her clothes and weapons.

Cle'or retrieved her throwing dagger from the body of the bowman who had tried to waylay her. She heard terrible cries from the stream then soon saw the falc flying overhead. An archer rose to Cle'or's left and sent an arrow at the shrieking bird. The shaft broke against her pale feathers. Before he could launch a second, he choked and stared at the hiltless dagger Cle'or had cast.

She heard swords clash and saw Fri'il clutching her livery to her with one hand and wielding her short sword in the other against a grim opponent who bled from three small wounds.

As he closed with her, she threw her livery at the man's feet. He tripped and she offered no mercy, though she made her attack quick. She stared down at him then took back her livery as Cle'or hurried to her.

"Are you all right?"

"There are two more back there," she replied.

"Like this one?"

"Wounded. I left one with both broken nose and knee. Raven bit the other one. I told him as she flew off that the bite contained a slow acting poison. They've fled off through the woods." At Cle'or's disapproving look, she muttered, "I couldn't kill them."

"But you could, now."

"I suppose so." She looked down at herself. "I had only time enough to find my short sword and this before this other was upon me."

"Come on, then!"

George and Se'and's conversation abruptly ended. George shook his head, slightly out of breath as Se'and shouldered him back at the sound of a bowstring's twang. Snapping out his hand, George mentally knocked the arrow away just before it would have reached her.

She unerringly cast a dagger. The bowman gasped, clutching at the arrow jutting from his throat. He swayed on his perch upon a sturdy tree branch then fell with a sickening thud.

Se'and glanced down at the arrow embedded at her feet, realizing she had been the arrow's intended target.

"This does nothing to change my mind," he muttered.

Looking about them she replied, "It is you who misunderstand. Neither have you changed my mind."

They approached their attacker. George half-saw movement in the trees.

'May I increase rapport now?' whispered the voice in his mind.

"Absolutely. Now, scan the area!"

Then they heard a falc's urgent cry. An image rose in George's mind. "Se'and, we've more than isolated trouble here."

She quickly retrieved her thrown dagger. "Our ill luck to have been found by brigands."

He wondered how much luck really had anything to do with it while Staff's scan revealed to him human-size heat signatures. He could feel their presence. "There are two more just ahead. Try not to kill them, Se'and."

She glared at him, knowing his aversion. "If they allow me to let them live, I shall."

He nodded and pulled his cloak closer about him. His hand grasped the staff tightly and he concentrated. The staff's glow formed a translucent shield of energy beside him. The shield reflected a shadowed version of his form. He focused on Se'and's image, which gradually appeared reflected in the field. She smiled and hurried into the brush. George would serve as bait. Staff glowed and Se'and's image appeared beside him.

Se'and looked at herself, looking back at her. "That'll do nicely."

Nodding, George began to run back toward the camp, two more brigand archers saw his indistinct form and Se'and's trapped reflection, thinking their quarry together. They rose and let fly shafts.

Balfour tried to reason with his captors. "You have us at a disadvantage, sir. If it is a matter of money or food, take what you want and leave us in peace. We mean you no ill."

"Oh, we shall, M'lord, we shall. However, you are what we came for. Leaving your friends in peace has never been part of the plan."

They heard a muffled cry then that of a shrieking bird, growing louder as it neared. The brigand realized something was amiss and glared at the elfblood mage. "No tricks, I said! Kill the woman!" he shouted at his comrades.

The falc burst out of the trees and targeted the nearest bowman as he drew to release his shaft even as Balfour protested and reached out his hand, focusing on the second man.

The man's bow snapped in half, the knocked and half-aimed arrow falling aside. His other bowman screamed as the great falc raked its talons across his face. He beat it back, then hurriedly drew and shot his arrow at it.

The leader of the brigands drew a dagger even as the arrow struck the bird squarely and broke as if striking the toughest steel. The falc was not even slowed as it dove upon him once more.

Me'oh had grabbed her dagger and leapt to bar the man's attack. He growled as he swept his blade forward. Desperate, he sought to close with the elfblood mage and end what he was sure was a spell wrought on his men.

She met his attack with practiced ease. He was not without skill. With his other hand he drew a second and longer blade and smiled grimly as he prepared to skewer her. Then he noted the elfblood's gaze meet his and abruptly found it difficult to breathe.

157

As he hesitated the woman attacked and he elected a feint that in his last moments of consciousness allowed him to break past and stab out with his blade at the woman.

Me'oh barely managed to twist out of its way and felt the nearness of its passage as the brigand reached Balfour, who glared at him defiantly, concentrating on mentally blocking the man's airways and bring unconsciousness.

The man's knife was the merest fraction from Balfour's chest. The brigand's gaze held a triumphant gleam.

Raven dove at the second bowman who had drawn his ragged looking sword and fended her off with it. As she flew into the air she saw Me'oh narrowly miss being struck as her attacker staggered past.

Raven flew hastily across the camp, abandoning her bleeding and exhausted attacker, and dove at the brigand leader. She knocked the man to the side and he flailed out his arm, touching her with his blade. She shrilled in agony then lost hold of her form. She fell, stunned, stumbling to the ground, once more a little girl.

Balfour felt Raven's anguish as he was knocked aside. He cried out, raising his hands to his ears at Raven's mind numbing mental scream. The brigand confusedly turned away from Balfour to see a naked girl tumble to the ground. He took a ragged breath, suddenly free of the elfblood's influence.

"Danvers, look out!" cried his companion whose bow had been broken.

Danvers' long brown hair and ragged beard swung about his head as he hurriedly ducked. Cle'or's thrown hiltless dagger scratched his arm, barely missing its mark as the mage's other black liveried defender returned running out of the trees. She glared at him and drew another blade as the bleeding bowman grabbed his fallen bow. Cle'or ignored him as she sought to race across the encampment. Danvers, gasping deep breaths, flung himself upon the dazed elfblood and held him to the ground as Me'oh rushed him.

The bowman anxiously drew back on the bow and readied to release, but hastily dove to the side as a young woman in blood stained livery leapt out of the forest beside him with a scream of rage. The other vagabond raced forward to defend him and met Fri'il's descending short sword.

Cle'or glanced back and cast her throwing knife at the bowman, who was hurriedly taking aim once more. He gasped and fell as one of her hiltless knives was driven in his upper arm. Cle'or saw the bowman's arrow arch toward her and dove aside, the arrow narrowly missing its target. Fri'il's blade clashed as she fought the remaining brigand, who gritted his teeth as she cut his forearm and ducked his lunge.

Angered, he ferociously rained blows upon her, which quickly brought the slight woman to her knees as she held her sword two handed. She dropped backward and rolled aside, his sword cleaving a clump of ground. She rose and charged him. He fell back a step.

"Enough! Or he dies!" Danvers shouted.

"No!" Me'oh shouted as she halted in place, her defense abruptly stymied.

Danvers had come up behind the dazed Balfour and placed his knife to his neck. Cle'or lowered her next readied knife as she came to her feet with a deadly glare. His surviving man held himself poised before Fri'il, who was perspiring hard.

"That's better now. Much better," Danvers said between panting.

Outside, Raven lay stunned; her head ringing as Staff mentally touched her. 'Look and listen for us, little one.'

She sighed, knowing that was the least she could do. As she laid waiting, she wondered what had hit her. She glanced at the blade in the brigand's hand and focused on the intricately wrought blade and noticed the rune carved along its length, then shivered at the enchanted weapon, which, if it had been marked for her, would have done more than disrupted her abilities.

Staff, beware the blade! she shouted mentally.

'Acknowledged.'

159

George was out of breath and a bit bruised. He had allowed several of the arrows to strike his cloak. The sight of them bouncing off had disconcerted his attackers, allowing Se'and to catch the first of them completely by surprise. His cloak had momentarily lost the image of brightly dyed wool and revealed the scaled leather of its original form.

Se'and crept upon the second archer as George marched blithely onward. That archer had targeted Se'and's image, which faded as the arrows clove it and whizzed past George. The man had loosed four arrows before he realized his companion had not fired a shot. Se'and raised his own companion's bow upon him and loosed a shaft.

The man fell, clutching his pierced shoulder. Se'and dropped the bow and raced toward him. George stunned him with a narrowed blast from staff before she ever had to use the knife in her hand. The woman had looked at him for a moment as he approached her.

"He's stunned. He'll offer no resistance for quite some time." She glanced at the man's shoulder, "You cauterized his wound."

"That arrow will be quite painful to remove but he will live," George said.

That, at least, seemed to please her as they delayed no longer and hurriedly returned to the encampment. George was winded from both the trek and from having had to maintain the energy field.

Raven's mental warning to Staff reached George as they cautiously approached the last line of trees around the camp. Staff's scan focused on the brigand's dagger, now held at Balfour's throat. "Se'and, we need a distraction."

She nodded grimly then moved off to the left. His enrapport senses probed the runes carved into the blade. He could sense its enchantment, but did not know its true purpose. He had a feeling, though, that they were about to find that out.

"Back away slowly, ladies," Danvers ordered. "Reesz! Huet! Disarm them!"

Fri'il knelt to put her short sword on the ground and was pushed forward at sword point to join Cle'or. The other bowman named Huet staggered after, his injury roughly bandaged.

"If you harm him, I'll kill you," Cle'or warned as she warily removed her weapons.

Danvers grinned, "I've no doubt you would certainly try. But fear not, I have no intention of killing him unless you force me to it. The mage is too valuable to waste." Raven groaned as she stirred. Danvers glanced at her. "Girl, or whatever you are, stay right there!" Raven shook her head as if trying to clear it and struggled to rise. "Tell her to stay right there, I say!"

Me'oh heard the sound first and quickly shouted at Raven, "Do as he says!"

Danvers turned in confusion as the horses stampeded into the camp. His men rushed to get out of the way. A blast of energy shot across the encampment, striking Danvers, who gasped. Me'oh, who was nearest, dove forward and knocked Balfour out of his dazed captor's grasp. Two more quick blasts flared and struck down his bandit companions as Se'and rode past, hurrying to herd back the unrestrained mounts.

As he slumped to the ground, Danvers saw a brown cloaked man march out of the trees, his wooden staff ablaze with light. He instantly realized his error; he had confused the elfblood for the mage. Cle'or leapt at him in his lapse of attention even as he cast his enchanted dagger weakly away from him.

The dagger's hilt bounced off Balfour's back. There was an instant flare of magic and Balfour's eyes closed and he slumped forward without a sound.

"No!" Cle'or screamed and punched Danvers repeatedly. Me'oh immediately sought Balfour's pulse; her own heart feeling like it had stopped in fright.

"Stop her! We need answers that only he may have!" George demanded as Se'and reined back, staring at the scene in horror.

Raven shimmered as she rose in beast form and charged Cle'or, knocking her backward as George raced forward and came to

Balfour's side. Me'oh rejoiced, hushed, "Thank the first Lords of Cathart, he's alive. Balfour, wake up. Come on, please wake up."

Taking a deep breath, George probed his friend's unconscious body. He seemed unhurt, even smiled ever so slightly.

'George, look at his eyes. He's in REM.'

George asked surprised, "He's asleep?"

'And having rather pleasant dreams.'

Breaking the contact, George opened his eyes and glanced away from his friend, "Me'oh, it's apparently only a sleep spell. Any ideas about how to break it?"

She looked at him long and hard, then glanced at Danvers, "He must know."

George nodded and rose to confront their unconscious prisoner.

"Let me go!" Cle'or raged, throwing off the tawny beast.

Se'and intervened, "Cle'or, he's alive! Didn't you hear them? It's only a sleep spell!"

Gazing back at her slumbering lord, Cle'or seemed to slowly regain her wits, then angrily cried, "Let me kill that barbarian!"

"No," George said, noting that Fri'il was watching in shock. "We need answers and he's our best source."

Cle'or glared at him and slumped her shoulders, "I failed."

"No, you did not. Balfour lives and while he lives the house endures," Se'and replied.

Taking a deep breath, Clc'or nodded.

George turned to her and offered her his arms, feeling her inner turmoil, seeing bits of recent memory. "It's all right. They were no match for you," he whispered to her softly.

She tried to hide her sudden tears as he softly hugged her. She remembered the brigand's filthy touch but took solace in what she had done to him, knowing he would likely limp for the rest of his life. Perhaps, Cle'or was right. Perhaps she should have killed him.

George turned her face toward him as if he had somehow heard her thoughts. "Fri'il, permanent harm to another can mar your life."

Pity him, but not yourself, whispered a strange voice in her mind, which she realized was the Summoning. *You are strong. Believe in yourself.*

Raven heard that voice and shimmered, returning to human form. Worried and uncertain, she gazed at their despair.

Danvers woke bound and hanging from a tree. His clothes were gone and there was no sign of his men. His head ached, filled with images of the tavern where he had accepted the commission for his now failure, and taken the enchanted blade.

His host had smiled, when he gave him the commission and said, "The full bounty for the mage alive. This dagger will spell him asleep, nothing more. Kill him and you get half. Either way, you and your friends make a profit."

"You really think he will come this far north?"

"Perhaps, who can be sure? There are only a limited number of ways to reach the Empire. The old Gate at Niota, though rarely traveled, is still an option for them. Yet know you are not the only troop to be hired. They will not be permitted to escape."

"If they come through my stretch of forest, I shall be the only one to collect your bounty."

The man smiled. "Just bring him here. Leave the rest to my master."

Danvers nodded and finished his drink, wondering at the strange light that seemed to dance before his eyes. A black liveried woman stood before him. "I told you that if you hurt my lord that I would kill you."

He felt as if he were floating from his memory as he beheld a dagger in her hand. She cast and he groaned in pain as it struck. She cast another, and another, as he screamed.

Horror overcame him as he woke bound and hanging from the tree. His head ached as he realized he was unhurt. He briefly remembered his bargain at the tavern, then there was light and the black liveried woman suddenly stood before him once more. "I told you that if you hurt my lord that I would kill you."

163

He gaped in horror as she cast the dagger, then another, and another.

His scream echoed through the night as Cle'or rode beside Me'oh who rode double, holding her sleeping lord soundly in her arms. She smiled.

Fri'il glanced at George. "Would not death have been better?"

George did not at first reply. He then answered, "And what lesson would have been learned?"

"His men would have learned fear."

Frowning, he said, "I am more concerned about the lesson you and I would have learned."

Se'and thought that perhaps her human mage husband may have understood more about being Cathartan from her tale of the Shattered House than she had dared hope. The screaming echoed once more as they rode throughout the night.

Chapter 21: Aslumber in Trelor

They paused and dismounted several miles from the edge of the woods. The short-haired Raven walked into the trees and, a moment later, tapped the special clasps at her shoulder. Her livery, which was the only thing she was willing to wear, dropped to the ground. She began running free and spread her arms and shimmered, changed. Raven, in the form of a large falc, burst upward into the air.

The blonde haired Fri'il retrieved Raven's livery, dusted it off, carefully folded it, and shook her head with a wistful smile. Her other companions began changing into the ragged clothes they had recently liberated from their previous owners.

Everyone was changing, that is, except for the snoring elfblooded Balfour, slumped with his hands and legs bound to his horse's saddle and stirrups. Me'oh paused, triple checking that the reins for his mount were secure. She had been riding behind him and couldn't help but think this was her fault.

Raven cawed as she saw the crossroads in the distance. George glanced up, then closed his eyes and saw what the were did. The sign on the road read "Trelor Six Leagues."

"Are you sure about this, Je'orj?" asked Se'and, setting her sword down and donning the jerkin over her black bodice.

George tossed his cloak to Me'oh to put on his sleeping friend. "Of course," he replied.

'George, based on her biometrics, she knows you're lying,' the staff in his hands whispered in his mind.

He grimaced. He didn't believe himself, either. After all, in the world he found himself, elvin magery ruled and only those with elvin blood could do magery. So why would anyone think for a second that a human could do magic? Well, try explaining that to people who didn't understand technology and science, as warped as they became in this place. Hence the bounty hunting bandits' mistake in targeting his elfblooded friend as the mage they were sent to collect.

George's plan was to walk into the lion's den to find the mage who enchanted the bespelled dagger that put Balfour to sleep. He

165

aimed to trick him into revealing how to break the spell. All he had to do was pretend to be a bounty hunter seeking his reward.

'You don't even know how you're going to break the spell once you find the mage, George.' Staff said to him across their mental link.

It's not like you've come up with a better idea, he thought, gripping his computer staff harder.

'I'm a computer. What do I know about magic?' it replied. It flashed the odds of success across his mind.

"Oh, thanks," he muttered.

'Just trying to be helpful.'

"Don't," he grumbled.

Se'and frowned as Cle'or and Fri'il, braided their hair and pulled it up under the worn and foul smelling caps the brigands who ambushed them had sported. They looked less feminine and wondered if their conscious adopted lord was having one of his spells again.

It was hard enough dealing with the dilemma of their sleeping elfblooded lord by bond, who Cle'or in particular felt was the easier to protect. George, with his worse than foreign ways, seemed intent on making things difficult. This was a task he should be letting her deal with. She smiled thinly at her own skills with a blade. She'd make the mage that had cast the spell reveal his secrets, magery or no.

George shook his head, having no doubt about what Cle'or was thinking. Since falling through the elvin gate, he'd learned how focused these bodyguards he had inherited were. No matter, they felt the bond made them family, and having the ladies watching his back was not as bad as he'd first thought…but he wasn't going to tell them that.

Cle'or argued to be allowed to deal with this herself as a matter of honor.

Cathartan honor be damned, George thought. *Those moments of conflict made him miss working a dig. It had been so much nicer imagining life in a distant time and place rather than living it.*

'If you discount the magic—'

"Stop listening to my thoughts, Staff."

'Sorry, lowering rapport level.'

George nodded, knowing it wouldn't be long before they reached the outskirts of the city-state, at which point he hoped his Cathartan bodyguards wouldn't have to kill anyone, nor would he.

'Don't count on it.'

"Lower the damned rapport level another fifty percent."

'You're no fun, George.'

Raven flew toward the dilapidated sprawl of buildings before the walls of Trelor. She couldn't help but think that should the city ever face attack it would be the city's poor, living outside the protection of the walls, who would suffer the most for it.

But such was life in the Crescent Lands, home to a number of city-states arching from the northern ridge of the Barrier Mountains to the ocean in the south, where lay the largest and wealthiest city-state, Hollif. However, Trelor had a rather unsavory reputation, and the flags flying over the city augured worse. If, at that moment, she had been human, she would have soured her expression.

'What's wrong?' Staff asked through their mental link.

She made no answer as she flew toward the nearest flag flapping in the breeze. It was not the flag of Trelor. She soared upward and scouted the city patrols, whose soldiers wore sashes over their chainmail. They were sashes with the same sigil as on the new flags flying over the city.

The well armed man in nondescript garb kept to the shadows and observed the tavern from the alley. Fenn du Blain had taken up residence here. It was an unlikely embassy, but Fenn liked playing with his food, which for some reason made those he ruled a bit uneasy. A blindfolded and shackled young woman was dragged to the rear entrance of the inn with the tavern on the main floor. She wasn't the first. He had seen children dragged inside the day before. That's how he knew Fenn was here.

The guards didn't dare hit her, but yanking her about served the guardsmen's purpose just as well. Fenn liked taking his time torturing his victims and a guard's body had been dumped outside, unceremoniously, just that morning. Apparently the guard had either shown signs of sympathy for Fenn's most recent victim or perhaps laughed a second too late for Fenn's liking.

He shook his head, knowing there was nothing he could do for Fenn's latest victims other than do the one thing he was destined to do: take back what was rightfully his. When he assured himself of his purpose was when he saw the falc flying overhead. His eyes widened for he knew such a sight was rare. Falcs were creatures of the Northlands. They roosted in the Imperial Cliffs and throughout what was termed the Gwed Mountains, which were actually the northern tip of the Barrier Mountain Chain that sheltered the border of the Eastern Northlands and the northern Crescent.

The Demonlord's minions seemed loath to disturb falcs. He didn't blame them. The birds were resistant to elvin magery and had very sharp talons. Only those who bonded to falcs, which most considered an act of madness, lived in harmony with their ilk. He watched the falc circle the tavern inn and couldn't help but think it an omen. The old banner of Gwed had been a falc rampant.

It was bad enough that du Blain's standard fluttered above this suborned city-state as it did above Gwed, itself. And, if Fenn du Blain had his way it would grace every city across the Crescent and the Northlands. He would create an empire that would rival Aqwaine but with darker goals, since the one thing du Blain worshipped was the Demonlord, himself.

So the falc, he thought, *was the sign he had been waiting for.* Tonight he would avenge his family, his people, and retrieve his stolen birthright.

Truthsayer stared as the prisoner was brought into Fenn's rooms. He did his best to ignore the piteous cries and moaning from the figures already tied face down upon the blood drenched bed.

"Well, well," Fenn said as the guard captain finished explaining how the prisoner had walked up to them and surrendered herself. "You can leave us but as a reward, take whomever pleases you downstairs. The night is yours."

"Thank you, M'lord!" the captain said, leading his men back outside.

Fenn's servant pulled off the woman's blindfold. She blinked and said, "As it is foretold, I come before you, Fenn du Blain."

Fenn glanced at his truthsayer, who nodded.

"Seeress, you've returned to your city at long last, I see," Fenn said with a cruel laugh.

"The time is now."

"And why is that?"

"I must do as the vision demands, Fenn," she replied.

"His title is Lord Fenn, woman!" the servant shouted, kicking her and knocking her to the floor.

She grunted, "Is that what those children call you?"

Fenn chuckled, "Sayer, is she speaking the truth?"

"Yes, M'lord," he replied, trying not to wince.

"Well, Seeress, since only these children are foolish enough to rebel against me, I've been teaching them that those who love their skin follow me, absolutely. Perhaps you'll enjoy the same lesson?"

The young woman's green-eyed gaze narrowed. She possessed the merest touch of elvin ancestry. She did not reply as Fenn gestured to his servant, who ripped the clothing off her back as Truthsayer begged his leave.

"Always so squeamish, old friend?"

Sayer nodded.

"Oh, leave us then," Fenn said. "Your attitude will spoil my fun without doubt."

Truthsayer met the woman's gaze, knowing it would forever haunt him as did so much else.

George glanced at Raven in falc form as she flew across the walled city. From his vantage he couldn't help but think of it as

169

vaguely medieval. It didn't have the old elvin character of the official buildings of Edous, the only city-state he had gotten a chance to observe, although observe wasn't precisely what others likely called it. The Demonlord was taking notice that his carefully stacked applecart was being overturned. The archeologist in him desperately wished he could scan the city and build an appropriate model for future reference, but that would certainly take time he could not afford, not if he wanted to save his friend.

However, that didn't mean he couldn't passively take the images Raven was relaying to his computer staff and match them with the probed memories of the bounty hunter, Danvers, specifically the keen recollection of where the brigand had gotten the enchanted blade used to put Balfour to sleep.

Raven banked, found the street, and circled the large inn Danvers visited, accepting the mission being offered to many willing thugs, who headed in all directions in pursuit of a foreign mage.

City guardsmen rode toward them as they approached the outer town. They took one look at the snoring elfblood and the ill dressed party and blocked their way.

The guards edged closer as if they planned to take credit for the capture, then Cle'or, Se'and, Me'oh, and Fri'il drew their swords.

George grimaced as he said, borrowing Danvers remembered diction. "Gentleman, we're all that's made it back. We earned ever silver!"

The sergeant gestured them to proceed. He and his mounted men followed behind.

Raven soared overhead as they headed directly toward the destination they were expected to know. George smiled as if delighted to soon be getting his reward. In a way, he would get a reward, though not one they expected, but certainly the one they deserved.

The tavern was filled with men rich or deadly, all here to fawn over the foreigner upstairs who had suborned the city's leadership and wealth. Truthsayer tossed down another drink and tried not to dwell on the occasional piercing scream that drew worried looks from the Trelorian rabble. It was bad enough that he helped Fenn to use truth against his enemies. He didn't want to dwell on the Seeress's eyes, knowing they saw into his soul.

"Another," he grunted, not offering to pay. It was the only perk he dared acknowledge since he had sold his soul to Fenn's venal will.

The man quickly obeyed, knowing that his life and limbs depended on it. To say a single word before Lord Fenn's soothsayer had been the undoing of several patrons.

There was a disturbance at the door.

"M'lord mage!" the guard sergeant shouted. "They brought the one you seek!"

Ayandre, Fenn's sycophant mage sat at the table in the far corner and clapped his hands, "Excellent!"

Truthsayer looked on as a snoring elfblood was dragged in by a pair of raggedly dressed brigands followed by three others. He sensed something wrong about them.

"We've come for the reward!" the man carrying the mage's staff shouted.

That's when every fiber of Truthsayer's being burned, LIE.

He met the liar's gaze and before he could shout a warning he felt something leap into him. His mouth snapped shut. *No, Truthsayer, you will not spoil this day. Truth shall win out.*

His eyes watered. He knew that elvin voice and began to tremble with shame.

Fenn bent and licked the tears from her face, "Is this the moment you saw in your dreams, Seeress?"

Her breath ragged from the pain.

"Yes," she muttered.

There was the knock she expected at the door.

Fenn rose, "What?!"

His servant went to the door, listened to the guard outside, and nodded, "M'lord...."

171

"Yes," she whispered, thinking this is exactly what she foresaw. Fenn left her and she strained to see the unconscious children across the room. *Soon,* she thought as her eyes sparkled with vision.

There were only two guards at the tavern's kitchen door. The sun was setting and attention was being drawn to the front of the inn as newcomers, apparently come for the bounty, approached. The guards were of Fenn's personal troops. Gwilliam needed to make their deaths quick and silent if he was to have any chance of success.

"No time like the present," he muttered as he left the alley, drawing a throwing dagger even as something dove silently from the sky and knocked the guards down. Instinctively, Gwilliam threw the dagger, taking out the nearest guard before he had a chance to rise.

The second guard made a rasping sound as he slumped backward as the falc hopped back on the ground and glanced at Gwilliam.

He raised his hand, "Wise one, I mean you no harm."

The pale falc with a black crest cocked its head then shimmered and changed into a tawny furred beast with a black mane before his widening eyes. It nodded toward the door.

"Well... I take it you're here to rescue your mage friend, then?"

The beast, which reminded him of a hellhound, nodded.

He chuckled, "Allow me, then."

He opened the door and watched his new found companion bound inside. Apparently the stars were aligning nicely this evening. "You're mine, Fenn," he muttered.

Fenn du Blain's pet mage, Ayandre, smiled and gestured for the snoring elfblooded mage to be brought before him. "Let us first see if you've brought me who we're paying for, my friend."

The man escorting the prize nodded as his companions set Balfour before him.

The mage rose and said, "That is his staff?"

"Aye, M'lord," the brigand leader replied, coming forward and offered the staff to him.

The mage reached to take it and no sooner had his fingers touched it than it twinkled.

'Engaging mind probe: locked on.'

He felt time slip, couldn't move, and heard another voice inside in his head. *'Ayandre, how does the sleep spell work?'*

The moment stretched as Ayandre found himself enchanted, his thoughts laid bare, his every evil, petty to major, revealed. The dagger sleep spell and its counter were presented.

The brigand smiled and spun his staff now tightly gripped in Ayandre's hand and grounded it against Balfour side.

The spell rebounded to its maker, who was blasted backward off his feet to the wall. He slammed against it then slumped to the floor.

The Cathartans drew their swords as George turned to the staring crowd, his staff ablaze with light.

George smiled and said into the stunned silence, "Now where can I find Fenn du Blain?"

"Right here!"

A bolt of power blasted down from the stairwell out of the hand of the elfblooded lord. The blast struck George's mental shield even as Fenn shouted, "Kill them!"

The patrons and guardsmen drew swords and daggers and charged forward even as the four Cathartans kicked chairs and tables to trip their assailants while knocking back their hated, itchy caps, freeing their braided hair.

Truthsayer looked for safety, realizing the mage's bodyguards were all women. Patrons clashed with them as the human mage positioned himself over the prone body of the still sleeping elfblood.

"Staff?" George muttered, wondering if he'd failed to break the spell.

'Scanning. Balfour's sleep patterns are returning to norms,' the computer replied.

The talisman hanging from Fenn's neck glowed red as he cast bolt after bolt of power at the human mage to no avail. "Very well," Fenn shouted with a grimace, "watch your companions die, then!" He turned and redirected his fire at Me'oh.

"Duck!" George shouted. He extended his glimmering shield as he saw Raven's pale fur appear in the shadows of the hallway behind Fenn.

Me'oh dove aside as the blast edged toward her and George sent power flaring to meet it, protecting her.

Fenn chose a new target and found himself suddenly knocked off his feet from behind. A beast growled and clawed at him. The guard behind him began to rush down the stairs but was suddenly grabbed from behind by a large man who clubbed him with the hilt of his sword.

Fenn was left to struggle with the beast. He blasted it, sending it sailing through the railing, never noticing the newcomer behind him.

Truthsayer dove behind the bar and heard a discordant whine. He paled at the sight of a face he never expected to see again.

The man grinned at him as he crept up on Fenn.

Don't, the voice returned.

Truthsayer cringed.

You can't save her.

He knew that and muttered, "How are you doing this?"

I've summoned the mage.

He knew there could be only one reason for invoking a Summoning. "You're dying," he muttered.

Sayer, for once you are going to honor the price for truth and not betray it, else I haunt you for the rest of your miserable life.

Cle'or blocked then lunged as Se'and stepped back and struck the guard sergeant on the back of the head. Cle'or's opponent, another guardsman, went down as Fri'il put her training to fine use and kicked one of the grimmer denizens between the legs. He groaned. She followed up by kneeing him in the head to bring him down.

"Good girl!" Cle'or yelled as she cast a dagger at a guard who hastily strung his bow. Her blade severed the string. The prospective bowman glanced at the grinning Cle'or and ducked out.

Fri'il charged the next two cutthroats as George sent more bolts of energy from his computer staff, which shattered tables, showering assailants with splinters. Dozens more chose the better part of valor and fled. Being around mages in a fight was never healthy for bystanders. The presence of Fenn du Blain only made matters worse.

Se'and saw Raven rising from where she had fallen. A swordsman thought to kill the beast only to have his blade bounce off her hide. George raised his staff high and sent a gust of wind that knocked the man off his feet and through the window that Fenn's personal troops were about to break through as the easiest egress under the circumstances. However, they were knocked backward as the window exploded in shards of glass scything through them.

Fenn struggled back to his feet when the sword nearly took off his head. There was a snick and he felt an explosion in his mind. Nearly blinded, he felt the chain holding his precious talisman slip off his shoulder and saw a large hand grab the darkening jewel. There was a flare of golden light as those fingers closed over it.

"Thank you, Fenn!"

His knees buckled as his vision cleared, "You!"

The exiled Gwilliam of Gwed, last member of the deposed royal family, grinned at him as he headed back up the stairs. "Send my regards to your beloved wife!"

Fenn cursed, struggling to chase Gwilliam even as his men below fell back in disarray. He saw the beast leap from floor to table, returning to him midway up the stairs.

Grimacing, he struggled with it as its jaws sought to close around his neck and its claws raked his ribs.

"No, Raven!" George shouted.

The beast's eyes lost their feral glint and Fenn thrust it aside and raced back up the stairs, shouting uselessly, "Kill them!"

Raven bolted after him. He glanced behind him and saw the linen chute. He raced to it and dove into it making his unceremonious escape, knowing that without the talisman his gifts were paltry.

He hit the cold stone floor hard and as he lost consciousness cursed himself a fool; the Seeress had known all along!

Gwilliam burst through the door to Fenn's rooms. Fenn's personal torturer, who doubled as body servant, was leaning over the Seeress and cutting the flesh off her back as she struggled not to scream. As the torturer gaped at Gwilliam in shock, Gwilliam stabbed and ran the man through. The torturer gasped as his bloody knife fell from his lifeless fingers.

The Seeress glanced back and said coldly, "Save the children. You've little time."

"What?"

"You've the power to heal them," she said. "You must take them with you."

"Seeress," the bound girl whimpered. "No, he must save you!"

"We're not important," the boy said.

"Heal them!" The Seeress ordered. "They are more important than they realize!"

The jewel glowing with golden light in his hand, he quickly went to the children and bathed them in its light.

Their flayed skin regrew as their bonds rusted and turned to dust. Every broken bone healed in almost an instant.

He cut the two children's bonds. "Don't let her die," the half naked girl begged as she struggled to sit up.

Gwilliam turned and rushed to the young woman's side.

"You must not save me," the Seeress whispered. "You must flee."

He held the talisman before her, "Sorry to disappoint you."

The talisman's glow bathed her as tears welled in her eyes. "Please, no," she begged as her body healed, unable to take her eyes off Gwilliam. "Please, let me die."

He couldn't. The talisman's glow faded and she felt feelings she could not name, then rose trying to cover herself with the rags of her blouse. "You should not have done that."

176

He had the children look for something to cover her. "Thanks are unnecessary."

The pair pulled off the fallen servant's livery and shirt, and offered them to the Seeress. The girl used the livery to cover herself.

She put on the shirt and shook her head, "You really shouldn't have done that."

"Why?" Gwilliam asked.

The Seeress found it difficult not to meet his honest gaze. "I'm going to break your heart," she lied.

"What?" he said as Raven entered as beast and scratched at the floor, urging them to follow.

"We must leave," the Seeress said, brushing past him.

Chapter 22: Truthsayer's Commands

Fenn's rich and deadly hangers-on and his guardsmen were all groaning or unconscious on the floor.

Balfour grunted, then yawned as he sat up. He looked around, "Uh, did I miss something?"

"Bal!" Me'oh shouted rushing to his side and knocked him over as she kissed him.

Cle'or sheathed her dagger and glanced out the broken window as Se'and said, "Lord Je'orj, you do have a plan for getting us back out of the city?"

He blinked, "Um, of course, I do. We're going to get back on our horses and run like hell."

"Actually, you will not need to do that," said an elfblood rising from behind the bar. "I'll make sure no one tries to stop you."

"And who might you be?" George asked.

"I am the Truthsayer of Gwed. I'm Fenn's lieutenant, and since he's not here, as far as everyone else is concerned, I'm in charge."

"Why would you help us?" George asked.

He trembled, glanced around and said, "Never anger a Summoning."

Now that was something George could understand.

Balfour rolled his eyes as Me'oh hugged him, "Will someone please tell me what's going on?"

George shook his head, "Later."

Raven bounded down the steps followed by a young woman and two oddly dressed children, along with the swordsman who had come to their aid.

"The Truthsayer cannot lie," the woman said. "In this you can trust him."

"Then we'd all best be going!" George said.

"What do you mean they escaped?!" Fenn shouted as the human healer put ointment on his many deep cuts.

"Truthsayer ordered everyone to make way, M'lord."

"What? When I get my hands on him I'll kill him!"

A captain of Fenn's knelt, not daring to look up from the floor, "Once they reached the eastern gate the Truthsayer told us where we could find you and for me to give you a message."

"Out with it!"

"He said he had it on rather good authority that the next time he saw you in the Crescent Lands you would die."

Fenn gasped incredulously. "Guards! Ready my carriage! We return to Gwed immediately and you, captain, track down Truthsayer, the Seeress, and Gwilliam of Gwed, and kill them!"

"But what of the human mage?"

"Others will deal with him." Without his talisman Fenn certainly couldn't. He then wondered how he could prevent his master's wrath. "Round up two thousand people. I want them executed to remind the populace that I am to be feared."

The captain stiffened, uncertain just what to say.

"Do you have a problem with that, Captain?"

"M'lord, the Truthsayer ordered the jails emptied and the prisoners exiled. He also ordered all the citizens of Trelortown, outside the gates, to abandon their homes."

"I take it they've all gone."

"Yes, M'lord, none would disobey your orders."

"Then gather the two thousand from the merchants, guilders, and the fine families of this foul city," Fenn ordered.

The captain saluted and left, thankful that the Truthsayer was no longer at Fenn's side. He smiled grimly. The greedy families that had handed over this city to Fenn's depredations would be winnowed as soon as Fenn was away. Perhaps he could change the course of this truly foul city, where an orphan like him could only find a home in the Guard and simply hope for justice.

George watched the column of refugees head south with many of the newly exiled former prisoners serving as guardsman and scouts. Truthsayer, Gwilliam, the Seeress, and the two children paused beside them.

Se'and watched the Seeress closely. "I take it you don't like what you see."

"Yours is a difficult road," the Seeress whispered.

"And yours?"

"I'm bound to Gwilliam, now."

Gwilliam turned and said, "What?"

The Seeress did not look at him as she replied, "You saved my life. Fate demands I aid you."

"Where will you go?" George asked.

Gwilliam replied, "I must retake my kingdom."

"Not yet," the Seeress replied. "If you try, you will fail, Gwilliam."

"Truth," Truthsayer heard himself say, then added, "Fenn's been raising an army. He sent Trelor's people to train under his officers. He means to take the whole of the Crescent and something more, which he was careful never to mention in my hearing out of fear I'd discern the truth.

Gwilliam looked to the Seeress. "So where must I go to succeed in taking back Gwed?"

The Seeress looked to the sky, "All I see is the place where you must raise your army, M'lord du Gwed." She pointed south.

"My army?"

She pointed. "Many will follow the falc's standard. You must warn the central and southern cities, though, few will listen."

"Me?" Gwilliam said.

The Seeress nodded, "And you, human mage, harbinger of change, must follow your Summoning and confront your fate."

Cle'or's hand moved unconsciously to her dagger. The Seeress glanced at her and met her gaze.

"You must watch your temper, m'lady. Yours is not the life you sought but it shall be more than you imagined. Many will underestimate you to their rue."

"And my house? Shall it thrive?" Cle'or asked.

The Seeress smiled, "As I said, many will underestimate you to their rue, m'lady." She departed without looking back, the pair of children running after her.

Fri'il became heated. "You aren't just going to leave it at that, are you?"

Cle'or chuckled, "Go ask her, yourself."

George reached out and blocked the young woman. "Fri'il, fate is what we make of it. You don't need a fortune teller to define you or any of us."

Me'oh looked for reassurance in Se'and. Me'oh canted her head then asked under her breath, "What's bothering you?"

"Did you notice how she wouldn't look at me?" Se'and answered.

"I noticed she wouldn't look at Fri'il, either, so?" Me'oh replied.

Se'and said, "She wouldn't look at Je'orj, either."

"If I were a seeress, the three of you would give me a headache, too," she responded with a chuckle.

Se'and wasn't amused.

'George,' Staff mentally said having enhanced his partner's hearing, 'I think Se'and is on to something '

"Yep, it gives me a headache, too," he muttered. "Now, shut up." He went over to his horse and mounted. "Are you all just going to stand there?"

His friends mounted as Raven circled overhead while Gwilliam's future army of men, women, and children headed south. George wished them luck in trying to get Edous to join their cause. At least they wouldn't have to contend with Raven's former master.

The Summoning watched and saw Truthsayer wince. *Yes, I'm still here*, it whispered.

"I've done all you asked!" he muttered, drawing an odd look from Gwilliam.

Not yet, you haven't.

Truthsayer glanced and thought about this penance for all the evils he had abetted and ones he committed that he shied from even thinking about. "What else?" he muttered under his breath.

The unicorn is seeking out the Hand.

Gwilliam glanced back as Truthsayer stood in his tracks. "Is there anything wrong, Sayer?"

"Uh, no, Gwill, I mean, M'lord."

"Sayer, don't play with half-truths. Your last one made me an exile."

"I'm sorry, Gwill. But you lived to fight another day."

He shook his head and asked, "Was it all worth it?"

"Selling my soul for the love of the woman who loved you, Gwill? No. I was a fool. But then again, so were you."

Gwilliam touched the talisman, "Well, this little lady more than makes up for it."

The Seeress walked ahead and shivered, hearing that conversation echo through her mind. The girl took hold of her hand, "Mistress?"

She looked at her future successor, "I'm fine, Vella. Are you all right?"

The girl frowned, glancing at her only remaining friend, unsure what to say.

The Seeress shook her head. "You already know."

"Oh."

The Seeress tried not to glance at Gwilliam and the girl's eyes widened. "Mistress?"

She paused. "Yes, I've got it badly. It would be better had he let me die."

The girl, last apprentice of the Temple of Trelor, gasped, knowing that Seeresses were warned about one thing. Falling in love could end foresight and would make their lovers' lives a living hell.

"Oh, mistress."

Yes, that sums it up nicely, the Seeress thought as her heart beat faster at the thought of Gwilliam. Her pleasant thoughts were pierced by the vision of George Bradley's cries of anguish that shattered through her.

Chapter 23: At Wit's End in Niota

Raslinn cast the bones, which rattled as they fell, rolling to a stop. He glanced at them then out the tower window and looked out over the Empire's edge, roiling with building gray clouds.

His thin fingered hands curled with anticipation and he slowly smiled. He read the augury and laughed, "Destiny conspires to bring you within my grasp, mageling. Your death is assured…and by such delicious means!"

His laughter echoed on the winds swirling past the ancient fastness's walls, which should have represented a defense of the Imperial plateau from attack from the lands far below.

The falc soared. Its keen sight noted every crag of the escarpment, rising high above the low lands, which stretched across the west like a wall. A narrow ledge snaked up its length, which was more path than road after long centuries of use. It led up the cliff face to an ancient Imperial fastness.

A moment later the bird's gaze turned directly below, encompassing six weary, mounted, travelers. They rode through the hills past still smoldering farms. Carrion birds fanned their wings, disturbed out of their inglorious repast by the intruders.

Fri'il, the youngest of the black liveried escort, hurriedly looked away and swallowed bile. After a moment, she bitterly asked, "How could an army march upon their own people like this?"

Balfour shook his head, his healing sense numbed by all the death permeating the air.

Cle'or rode protectively closer to him and frowned, quietly fuming at the young woman's show of weakness and signed, *'No questions.'*

Me'oh, Balfour's other protector, glanced back at her reassuringly. Fri'il nodded and understood, then glanced up at the falc flying overhead. She saw the bird circle and gazed at George, who had not said a word since they had entered this region.

George sighed and held out his staff; the falc dived then hastily back-winged before settling upon the proffered perch. The impact was jarring.

The bird squawked indignantly, continuing to flap her wings, as the nearest horse grew uneasy.

"Raven, hop down," he urged, knowing she was too heavy for such antics.

Balfour shook his head at the falc's antics, his spirits momentarily lifted as he saw the staff glowing with a flickering light and heard it mentally whisper to her, *'I am not altogether comfortable serving as a perch. So, if you would be so kind?'*

Squawking for a second time, the falc edged closer to George and to shimmer as it hopped into his lap. Se'and reached back into her saddlebags and prepared herself for her lord's certain to follow shout.

"Se'and!" It came as the falc's shape shift was completed, leaving a naked black-haired little girl sitting before him.

His foster daughter seemed oblivious to his chagrin as Se'and rode forward and handed over the girl's clothing.

"Raven, please put this on."

"No!" she rasped angrily. "No want!"

The set of black livery was a hand-me-down from Fri'il and the only garment that Raven had been coaxed into wearing since being freed of the enchantment, which had permanently locked her into animal and bird forms.

"Put it on," George said.

"Don't want to," she replied imploringly, looking over her shoulder at him.

He gave her a one armed hug.

"Just as Staff does not appreciate being used as a perch, you know I do not appreciate your going without clothes when in human form."

"I still ride with you?" she asked hesitantly.

"Of course, little one."

185

She sighed and pulled the livery over her head, ignoring Se'and's grin. It was hard for George not to hear the woman's errant thought, *Ah, my lord so enjoys family life.*

Coughing hastily, he then inquired, "Raven, did you see any place you thought safe enough to lodge tonight?"

She nodded then pointed. "Barn safest. Storm coming."

Balfour looked at the clear sky. "What storm? The weather's perfect."

Doubtful, George raised his staff and closed his eyes. He opened himself to rapport and the computer staff glowed. He muttered, "Scan."

'Acknowledged. Scanning. Air pressure dropping.'

Data flooded George's mind. A front was moving in quickly although its presence was not yet visible.

Raven smugly smiled. "Storm! Staff agrees!"

The computer staff's data did not fit normal weather patterns. When George opened his eyes, he was anxious and worried. "Something's wrong about that storm. We had best find that shelter, quickly!"

They spurred their mounts and took off at a gallop.

Long before they reached the barn, the sky filled with dark clouds. Thunder cracked and a heavy wind stirred. The rain struck just as they reached the abandoned barn's sanctuary and drenched them instantly.

Cle'or and Fri'il fought to close the doors as the rest of the group hastily entered the structure. The wind nearly pulled the doors out of their hands. Me'oh quickly brought over the thick wooden bar and wrested it into place. The entire structure shook with the force of the rain and wind as George hurriedly dismounted and raised the staff high above his head. Blue warding light flared. Instantly the howl of the storm outside diminished.

Se'and hurried to his side as he swayed. "Are you all right, Je'orj?"

"Fine," he gasped, feeling the winds pound on the barrier he had raised. Balfour hurried to his other side as he abruptly slumped.

"Sure you're fine, my friend," Balfour murmured as they helped him to sit down. "Staff, I would like a status report, please."

The glowing staff linked to him and acknowledged. 'The storm matches no natural patterns. It is focusing its effects here.'

Lightning flared and struck the warding, once, then twice. George groaned and lost consciousness.

"Balfour!" Se'and exclaimed.

"I know!" he responded as the computer staff flared to blinding intensity.

'Rapport level increased as directed. George cannot long maintain this level without damage.'

Distantly, Balfour heard George's response, *'Maintain.'*

Balfour sighed and opened his eyes and saw the tense faces all around him. Muted thunder echoed around them. "Gee-orj is going to be stubborn about this."

Se'and glared at her sisters, "Of course, he is... So, how can we help?"

The storm raged and at some point seemed to call his name. It knew him and dimly he recognized it as well. The Summoning had brought him to this world of elvin magery where technology had been lost and the laws of science were blunted. The Summoning, which drew him toward the Empire, now seemed desperate to turn him aside.

There was another force equally insistent, demanding he enter the Empire most expediently. It called to him in a way the Summoning never had and told him the way home lay closer than he had ever imagined.

Fri'il hugged George close as he slept. He was growing cold and she was doing her best to warm him as Se'and and Me'oh hunted up all the blankets they could find.

Balfour looked about them uncertainly as the storm continued to rage. He could almost sense the true nature of the magery that brought it down upon them.

Raven sniffed the air and growled.

Balfour glanced at the girl as she took off her garment and set it down upon the other blankets. She then looked about her and growled again.

"Raven, what's wrong?"

"Fighting!" She exclaimed.

"Where? Is Gee-orj fighting someone?"

She shook her head. "Not him! Fighting…," she struggled to find the words, "…over him!" she exclaimed, pointing at her foster father.

Se'and lay down the last of the blankets as Balfour stared as Raven shimmered and became a tawny furred beast.

"Fighting," he muttered as Se'and disrobed and burrowed under the blankets to her lord's side. The staff was blazing bright.

Fri'il barely heard as she nestled as close as she could, then quickly kissed George on the neck. She knew he thought her little more than a child, but she was a full grown woman and just as Se'and was, his wife by bond, sworn to protect him with her very life if necessary.

The storm raged through the night. The staff's glow grew fainter as time passed. George weakly groaned every time lightning struck the protective field about the barn.

When the storm finally passed the next morning, George could barely be roused. Balfour had hardly slept at all during Cle'or's watch. When it was Me'oh's turn, Cle'or crawled into her bedroll and quickly fell asleep.

She had the strangest dream. An old elf was in the barn with them. He knelt worriedly by George's side while haunting laughter echoed in the buffeting wind outside and through the thunder. The elf looked desperately about, then saw her looking at him and stared at her in surprise.

"You can see me?"

"Who are you?" she heard herself say in her dream.

He hesitated, "You can hear me as well?"

Her dream self nodded.

He sighed, "Thank the Gate, not all is lost! I mean you no harm yet I am inadvertently causing him great pain! This storm is partly my fault but I have only been trying to protect him, I assure you!"

"That is our job, no one else's," she replied warningly.

The old elf blinked thoughtfully. "I know that. At least I think I did, once. It's so hard to keep things straight sometimes. Things are so different now. His mere presence has changed more than I dared hope. Perhaps, it is best that he walks into the trap so long as I can safeguard him through you."

Cle'or fingered her dagger. "Trap?"

The old elf walked toward her and reached out his hand. "Will you trust me?"

"Who are you?" she asked again.

He nodded, "I am an echo of the person I was, a shadow of myself. I am the Summoning. I must bring Gee-orj Bradlei to me and set all things right."

She let loose her dagger. His gaze seemed so old and tired yet kindly.

"You must take this," he gestured to George's discolored dagger, unable to touch it himself. She knelt and took it warily, uncertain whether a dream could be trusted. The old elf nodded and instantly faded away.

Waking with a start, she felt momentarily dizzy. Me'oh opened the barn doors on the misty morning then turned her head and heard Se'and and Balfour decide that they would hasten up the old escarpment path to Niota. She trembled in foreboding, and instinctively reached for her dagger. With an indrawn breath, she stared. George's dagger was in her hand. She quickly hid it, knowing that she was going to need it.

"As I've said before, I've been to Niota," Balfour stated. "We need to warn the Imperial forces there about Fenn du Blain's takeover of Trelor. Niota's our best chance, if we can keep away from du Blain's marauding army."

All agreed but there was still the matter of George. He was in no condition to leave. Se'and turned and knelt beside her sleeping lord. Much of his color was back. With the passing of the storm his staff had gone quiescent. Fri'il blinked her eyes and awoke. Se'and looked at her as she gently shook George.

He softly groaned and slowly opened his eyes, looking dazed. "M'lord, we have no choice but to make the ascent."

Blearily, he muttered, "What?"

"If we are to shake any pursuit, we must take the chance on entering the Empire from here."

The imperative struck him. He grunted with the pain.

Must ascend, a voice whispered in his mind.

"Must ascend," he heard himself weakly echo, not considering the fact that the Summoning had never before commanded him like this before.

Fri'il momentarily clung tighter to him as Se'and nodded, "We need to move on as soon as possible."

George weakly nodded and pulled away from the young woman at his side. She helped him sit up. He brusquely shook himself free of her help.

"I can do it," he muttered. He looked to his staff, which stood unaided several feet away.

Raven had rested in beast form throughout the night and woke to see Fri'il quickly turn away, trying to hide her tears. She saw Staff flicker with light and heard it communicate warnings. *'Interference detected.'*

George reached for the staff and Raven noted an odd shimmer. She heard Staff report, *'Likely caused by residual effects from the storm. Rapport to minimum levels.'*

As Fri'il helped Me'oh and the others pack their things, Raven padded outside the barn. The ground all about them looked devastated by the storm's fury. She sniffed the air, wary, then bounded around the barn in search of any sign of what she was sensing. She found nothing.

Se'and pulled on her mount's reins and looked up at the cliff-face. It was said that the Imperial mages long ago raised the very earth of the Empire as the ultimate defense against the Demonlord. Months before she had accompanied her sire and brother up the Imperial Road into the Empire, but that entrance led up into the Province of Rian, which lay far to the south and was a less daunting ascent than this ancient and narrow route into the Empire.

Fri'il steadied George in the saddle they now shared as he swayed. He was still weak from the deep rapport and they were all worried he might fall. Se'and took the lead, followed by George and Fri'il, then by Me'oh who rode before Balfour. Cle'or brought up the rear with the spare mounts. Raven chose to bound up the path well ahead of them and scout the way.

Se'and gestured and they began the ascent.

How long they ascended, George was uncertain. His staff was bound to his saddle and rested beside his knee. He only sensed that they traveled and Fri'il was talking to him quietly. He heard her distantly say something about "healthy daughters," but understood little of it. It was enough of a nuisance that Fri'il held on to him tightly and that the computer staff was helping him keep his balance.

He muttered some reply to her as she hugged him closer. He shook his head to clear it. *What was she saying to him? Why was he having so much trouble concentrating? He normally would have asked the computer staff, but for some reason that option did not occur to him.*

Fri'il pressed her cheek to George's back. He seemed to her to be recovering physically. She was growing terribly disturbed about one aspect of their relationship: the serious lack of one.

In her homeland there were few men. Those that did live there were either lords or sailors. Few of the foreign men ever stayed. Although Cathartan goods were prized and brought good prices in foreign markets, Cathartan ways were difficult for foreigners to

191

understand. Thousands of women of Cathart were craftsmen and artisans, merchants, farmers, fishermen, teachers and healers. They were also excellent bodyguards and soldiers, who allowed nothing to harm their people. Many outsiders learned that lesson rather forcefully. The luckier of repeat offenders were permanently banned from ever returning.

The one thing the women of Cathart most desired were to bear sons, healthy and strong. It was the Curse of their land that but one boy per household was ever born in a generation. The loss of even one sire and the consequences to the continued existence of humanity in Cathart could be devastating.

Thus, it was difficult for her Fri'il to fully understand George. But George knew not the intimate history of his escorts. Sire Ryff's son, Vyss, who had been dying when Balfour and George found them encamped on the Caravan Road, was Fri'il's affianced husband. As a secondson, Vyss was a rarity; a second born son to a Cathartan lord was considered a great blessing. A secondson did not inherit the full estate of a sire, after his passing, however. To establish a secondson's house, gifts of wives and property were traditionally provided from every house. As Vyss entered adolescence, the Curse's virulent form struck. On the date of his majority, when Vyss should have begun receiving his secondson gifts, only one lord honored the tradition. It was understandable, since no one had ever survived the Curse that, the Lords of Cathart declined to attend his being presented and to present him their due. Only Fri'il's sire had been faithful to the tradition and gifted Vyss a daughter in marriage. The lad was years her junior, yet had he been able, she would have proudly bore him children.

Throughout his illness, she had cared for and protected him as the first wife of his house. It was strange how strongly she had come to love him, realizing it most poignantly the moment Vyss presented her by bond. Not to be outdone by his father's generosity, Vyss had explained to her that he needed to reward the pair for saving his life as well. She understood that, it had been hard to accept that she was being given away. However, such were the duties of Cathartan life that she obeyed. She just had not expected to fall in love with her new lord.

"M'lord?" she said.

George grunted.

"I… I just want you to know that I would be proud to bear you strong healthy daughters."

His lack of response did not surprise her. He had made it plain that he did not intend to exercise his full rights as Fri'il's and Se'and's lord husband by bond. His ways were not their ways.

She sighed and got up her courage, "I do not believe it would be a… a burden, M'lord. It is just our way."

His head leaned further forward and she hugged him more tightly as their mount continued to plod up the path.

"You are not the only one far from home in a strange land, Je'orj. Se'and and I are your family now. We can make a fine home for you, a house full of strong daughters. You have seen that as protectors we are without equal. Cle'or says that my sword skills are shaping up nicely. I am not a child, Je'orj. I can make a fine home for you. I know I can!"

She sighed in frustration as his silence lengthened, then snuggled her check closer to his neck and whispered, "I am a woman, full grown."

She heard him grunt, which was likely the closest acknowledgement she would get.

The wind became fierce as they struggled forward until they reached the first wayfarer's camp. The area was a cavern carved into the cliff face. It was one of several along the path, which afforded vital resting places. The cavern was very large and provided more than enough space for all to dismount and rest.

Se'and unhappily noted that Fri'il seemed almost as pale as George. "You look exhausted. Get some sleep. Do want me to ride with him tomorrow?"

"No!" she hastily replied, then thought to explain. "It's difficult, but I'm managing well enough."

Nodding, Se'and wondered if she should not have pushed the issue further, then turned to other concerns. She hoped they would reach the safety of Niota quickly. The strain was wearing on them all. Perhaps after a good night's sleep, even with the wind howling outside, things would all be better.

"He will never love you," whispered the voice in Fri'il's dreams. "He means to leave you. You know that in your heart."

George now lay in her arms.

"He loves me!" she cried in her dream.

"Loves you? He is not capable of it. Only in Cathart will you ever find the love you crave. He is a man of another world and has no desire to sire a House. Se'and knows this. So why delude yourself? You are young and beautiful. Why should you swoon over a husband in a loveless bond?"

Tears welled. She knew it was true, every word.

George struggled to awaken, his head aching as if the Summoning were at war with itself. As Fri'il's tears touched his cheek, his eyes abruptly opened, but his gaze saw another place, a place of stone walls, gray and foreboding. There Fri'il stood, facing him with a knife, preparing to kill him. Behind her a black cloaked figure crooned encouragement, waving George's staff over his head.

George fought to wake, even as the computer staff in his nightmare flared with a grim light. It reached out to him, calling irresistibly. All the while Fri'il stood poised, uncertain.

"You must love me!" she pleaded.

When he gave no answer, cringing from the fey light, she screamed and lunged at him. Dark laughter echoed all around them.

Raven led the way as they started out the next morning. She was followed by Me'oh, then Balfour, then Fri'il. Se'and rode double with George, a decision she made after seeing how tired Fri'il had seemed after an apparently difficult night's sleep. The young woman's irritability only made her decision that much easier.

194

Cle'or rode rearguard. No one had often glanced at her seemingly from the moment they had begun their trek. The path was barely wide enough in places for even a single rider, though at intervals it widened enough for them to pause and rest as a group. Such halts never lasted long. Balfour checked on George and shook his head worriedly at Se'and. That, alone, should have been the reason for their feeling of urgency.

But Se'and felt there was something more, something ominous, so she brooked no delays. They quickly remounted and pushed on.

While Balfour rode he thought back upon his time at Niota so many years before. It had briefly served as a sanctuary. Raslinn, Lord of Niota, had offered him solace, telling him not to consider himself a failure just because he had been unable to effect the simplest of healing mageries.

Finally, when they came within sight of the keep's high white walls, majestic towers, and gleaming parapet, they couldn't help but think it was the most beautiful sight they had ever seen. The guards opened the gates for them at their approach and helped them from their mounts. Balfour tiredly noticed that all his companions were warmly greeted and were being made truly welcome.

Cle'or quickly dismounted. She saw each of her companions slumping forward as they entered the gates. She felt a terrible sense of urgency. She walked in her horse's shadow as folk in ragged dress helped their charges dismount then urged them into the main building.

Every instinct told her to defend Balfour and George; however, that other presence whispered in her mind that that would prove to be in vain. Strangely, no one seemed to notice her as she followed the mounts into the safety of the barn.

Se'and was awed by the magnificent hall. Marble arches gleamed and the chandeliers slowly revolved casting rainbow hues of light, which bathed the chamber.

"Ah, our guests must be made welcome! Bring food and drink while suitable rooms are prepared!" shouted the elvin lord of the keep.

Balfour saw the old silver-haired elf and smiled. "Lord Raslinn, it is so wonderful to see you again!"

The elf blinked and slowly grinned in recognition, "Young Balfour! So formal? My friend, I'm so happy to see you return to the Empire as I had always hoped!"

"Lord Raslinn," Balfour said, "my friend here has taken seriously ill."

"Ah, say no more," the elvin lord turned to his servants. "Take the gentleman directly to a guest room. I am sorry but I have no healer here, as you must remember."

"What ails my friend should react well enough to merely being within the Imperial wards here."

The old elf's expression changed from joy to deep concern. "Then the matter is more serious than mere sickness. Darkest magery must be afoot."

Balfour nodded. "Since I was last here, I have become a healer and could do nothing for him outside the boundary." Balfour suddenly felt lethargic and drained. His head slumped forward.

"Your journey up the escarpment has obviously taxed your strength. Take our guests directly to their rooms, then send up refreshments." The servants hastened off. Se'and and her fellow sisters were feeling a bit tired themselves and were only too happy to be led upstairs as well.

"You are most kind," Balfour muttered.

"Think nothing of it," Niota's lord replied, his gaze sparkling with ensorcellment, which made Balfour and the others see themselves being led to rooms where they might rest. In truth, his servants lifted each half-conscious, bespelled victim from his presence.

Cle'or hid in the unswept barn, which served as the keep's stables. Their horses had been unsaddled but had not been fed before

196

the servants quickly left. Minutes dragged by before she heard any further human movement.

Children dressed in rags, which appeared to have at one time been Imperial livery, entered the barn. They spoke not a word to one another. They merely provided the horses with feed and water.

From Cle'or's vantage she noticed water being taken into an apparently empty far stall and heard a brief muttered conversation. A child hastened out of the stall with a backward glance as the other children quickly left.

Over the sound of the horses eating Cle'or heard a gentle sobbing. She came out of hiding with her sword drawn and moved stealthily toward that end stall. When she looked within she saw a bruised and battered boy chained to the wall.

He glanced up with tears smearing his dirt encrusted face as he rasped, "I won't let you! Go away! Just leave me alone!"

Her hand trembled as she reached out to him, "Shh, little one, I will not harm you."

He blinked back his tears, then stared at her. "I don't know you. You must leave! Get as far away from here as fast as you can!"

"I cannot. My friends are here and they're in trouble," she replied quietly.

Sighing, the boy shook his head, "It is already too late for them as it is for all the rest of us here."

Someone entered the barn, "Thomi, have you learned your lesson?"

"Go, hurry!" he whispered.

Cle'or slipped under the wooden slats to the next stall as a woman bearing a bucket of water approached. "You're filthy child. Master wants you cleaned up. He has plans for you."

The lad cringed, then she dumped the bucket's contents over him. "I won't do it!" he cried.

"You will or the master says that he'll see you served as your friend's dinner!"

Thomi blanched, "Leave him alone!"

"He hasn't eaten ever since the master put you here. Do you really think he'll be able to help himself in a few more days? No? Then do what you're told!" She pinched his thin arm, "No doubt, the master will at last have to feed you proper, first."

The woman ripped the tattered jerkin from the boy's still defiant shoulders. She reached over and took down a whip.

"Thomi, you will obey!"

The sight of the whip being raised set Cle'or into motion; boys meant the very survival of her people. She cast two daggers. The first knocked the whip from the woman's stung fingers and the hilt of the second hit her squarely between the eyes.

She fell with a stunned groan. Thomi stood shocked at the scene as Cle'or came out of hiding.

"You didn't hurt my mother, did you?"

Cle'or blinked in confusion. *What kind of place was this?*

Chapter 24: Cages

Se'and awoke lying in a small metal cage. It gave her barely enough room to sit up. Straw covered the floor, making her itch.

"You're awake. I was growing worried."

She glanced back at Balfour, "What's happened?"

He shrugged, "What do you think, Me'oh?"

No matter how hard Se'and tried to crane her neck, the older Cathartan was out of her line of sight.

Me'oh chuckled grimly, "We've walked right into a trap again."

"Where are you?" Se'and muttered.

"Up here, hanging from the ceiling."

"Je'orj?"

"We're the only ones in here," Balfour concluded. "Wish I knew how this happened. Lord Raslinn was so kind to me when I was here before."

Se'and grimaced, "Are you sure?"

"What do you mean?"

"Think back. Was he really so kind to you?"

Balfour hastily replied, "Of course, he was!" His vehemence surprised him. He took a deep breath and concentrated. A wave of dizziness filled him, leaving him confused, uncertain what he was trying to do.

Me'oh saw his reaction and nodded, "Se'and, you're right. He's been bespelled with a false memory."

"What are you talking about?" he rasped.

Se'and shook her head, "Likely your every memory of your visit through here is false. If Je'orj were here he would likely tell you to just keep repeating that to yourself."

He shrugged, feeling dizzy again. He hardly heard her, the word false ringing through his mind. "False?" he muttered, then his eyes widened in anger. "False. False memories! How dare he?!" He had a sudden terrible headache. "False memory," he mumbled.

Me'oh shouted at him, "Balfour, are you all right?"

He slumped forward, then shook his head, "I... I remember. Oh, my, I remember it all."

There was laughter as the door opened, "Delightful! You've broken the enchantment! I must admit that that is quite impressive. None who have traveled this way ever have."

Balfour stared at Lord Raslinn and, for the first time, saw him as he truly appeared. He was no elf. The sallow skinned, pointy-eared, seven-foot-tall goblin chuckled mockingly. "You told me so much of the goings on at the capital, and your story of failure was so sad. At the time I chose to release you, my sole concern was not wanting to draw undue attention to my activities here. I could not imagine such a valueless miserable creature having any value. How ironic! Here you've brought me my master's greatest desire."

Se'and quietly tested the bars that caged her as their enemy continued to gloat.

"The death of the human mage will be so sweet added to my part in the coming invasion! Guards, take this one to the gallery!"

Her cage was roughly hefted and carried out as Balfour shouted, "Let her go!"

The goblin mage laughed, "Oh, you shall have your turn later!"

George jerked, awakening with a start. He lay in a sumptuous bed, but had no idea how he had come to be here. Then Fri'il entered carrying a tray of food.

"Oh, you're awake. We were getting worried."

"Where are we?" he asked.

"Niota, the keep at the edge of the Empire. Don't you remember?"

Bleary, he shook his head. "Where are Se'and and the others?"

"Eating dinner." She sat beside him and offered him a drink. The beverage was refreshingly tart, reminding him of a favorite drink he had not had in a very long time. Abruptly, he felt dizzy and lay back. *There was something else he should remember, but what was it? It was so strange.* He felt terribly tired.

Fri'il smiled warmly, her gaze slightly out of focus.

Thomi chafed his wrists as he limped along at Cle'or's side. "Is there another way inside?" Cle'or asked.

"When my mother does not return, they will send someone else. You must leave this wicked place!"

Cle'or paused beside him. "Listen, Thomi, my friends are in trouble. If I don't help them no one will."

A bell was rung and raggedly dressed people, young and old, hurried toward the main hall across the courtyard. Trembling, the boy gestured toward the sound.

"You hear that? They are already as good as dead."

She shook his shoulders, "Just tell me how to get inside without attracting attention. I will do the rest."

Grimly, he took her hand and led her, "There is only one way I can think of, but your only chance is if I'm with you."

Thomi took her to the rubble of a fallen building and they were able to slip past a broken doorway by crouching. Torches bracketed one wall and Cle'or lit one then followed Thomi into the dark corridor.

After a time they reached an intersecting passage. Something growled in the darkness as Cle'or drew her sword and spun to confront it. A massive arm pushed her back, sending her sprawling. It shambled forward as Thomi shouted, "No, Walsh! It's all right! She means you no harm!"

Cle'or gaped as the hulking eight-foot-tall ogre paused and turned to the boy, then smiled crookedly, "Tho-mi?"

"It's me, Walsh! She rescued me!"

The ogre gave a sob and brokenly explained, "Mara... said... master... kill...you...unless...'

"I know that, Walsh!"

The ogre quickly lifted the boy off the ground and hugged him. "Tho-mi...live. Only friend...not...die."

To Cle'or's astonishment, Thomi fervently hugged the creature back. The ogre gave a soft croon of pleasure. "Put me down now, Walsh. My new friend and I must get into the hall to try and save her friends!"

A bell rang out again and immediately the ogre stiffened and set the boy down. "He…summons." His gaze grew distant. "He…wants me kill." The ogre shook himself, "Tho–mi…must go! Not safe!"

The bell echoed once more and the ogre took an involuntary step away, then another. The boy took Cle'or's hand and led her down the passage opposite the retreating ogre. There were tears in his eyes. "We must hurry! There is little time!"

"What do you mean that he's gone?" Raslinn rasped at the cowered woman, Mara, who sported a sizeable bump on her head.

"I went as you commanded, Master! Then I was knocked unconscious!"

"Fool! Guards! Find Thomi! I'll not have this spectacle ruined!" Then he looked at the woman darkly. "Your punishment should, at least, prove amusing."

Raven blinked sleep from her eyes, no longer in human form, but in her beast shape. About her neck she wore a jeweled collar. She tried to shake it off, then willed herself to change but nothing happened.

Light suddenly filled the pit around her. The walls were lined with seated people, staring at her in fascination. She heard a grim laugh then saw the goblin come into the light.

"You are collared to our dark master's will once more, were-child!"

Raven growled at Raslinn.

"You will do my will! And since you must be famished, here is a morsel for you."

He drew a frightened woman up beside him and callously tossed her screaming into the pit. "Enjoy!" he shouted and turned to the staring, raggedly dressed crowd, who abruptly applauded.

"Good, that's better," he preened. "That should teach the dratted boy the price of daring to disobey me."

Cle'or and Thomi heard the screaming as they came out behind the seats lining the pit. Thomi stared from their vantage in horror. Cle'or's gaze narrowed as Raven, in beast form, shuddered and rose at the sight of the terrified woman.

Raven growled, then took half a step forward before twisting about, fighting the geas placed upon her.

Raslinn shook his head, "This will not do at all." He raised his left hand. "Lower it!"

There was a creaking noise from high above. Cle'or watched a cage bearing Se'and swaying into the light.

"This should serve as incentive, my pet! Now, kill the morsel before you!"

Raven howled and bit at the air.

A stooped old man guarded the door to the others' cell. Balfour closed his eyes and mentally reached out to him. The man suddenly began breathing hard, then glanced sheepishly into the room. He looked up at Me'oh and muttered, "My, my, what a lovely specimen."

He took his key and opened the door. The old fellow's face was flush as he entered. His clawing hands reached for Me'oh's ankle. She kicked at him.

"Feisty. I like that."

Me'oh glanced at Balfour and frowned, noting his deep look of concentration. She suddenly smiled, "You want me? That's too bad since I'm locked in here."

"So? I've the key?" he held it up. "Just promise me a kiss?"

She grinned, "Just a kiss?"

He hurriedly put the key in the lock and turned it. Me'oh kicked outward sending him sprawling. He shook his head to clear his addled wits. "What am I thinking?" he muttered.

"Sleep now," Balfour whispered in answer. The man's eyes shut and he slumped to the floor snoring lightly. Balfour opened his eyes as Me'oh hastened from her cage and grabbed the key.

"Give a girl some warning next time," Me'oh said.

Balfour took a deep calming breath, "Nice work."

Moments later they were both free. Me'oh thoughtfully closed the cell door behind them, wishing the man well in his slumber.

Raven raced forward and swatted her prey. The woman cried out in fear, "Please, master, no!"

"This is the boy's fault! You knew what I wanted from him and you let him escape!" he responded.

Raven leapt. The woman fell backwards as Raven's gaping jaws snapped just inches from her throat.

She struggled to fend off the beast. "No! Please!"

Intelligence flashed in Raven's eyes and she turned her gnashing teeth to the side.

Thomi stepped into the light and faced the goblin, "You wanted me here?"

Raslinn stared incredulous, raised his hand, and muttered a half-heard word. The geas instantly restrained Raven's attack. "Who freed you?"

Thomi laughed, "What? You didn't appreciate my little trick?"

"Boy, do you want to join her?" the goblin mage shouted.

"Release my mother and I'll order Walsh to obey you."

The goblin glared at him, then shouted, "Throw down a rope, then make ready to release the ogre. The main event is about to commence!"

Thomi took a deep breath as his mother was helped from the pit. He then looked worriedly across its length. A thick wooden door was raised. The ogre stepped into the pit and saw the waiting pale beast with a black mane.

Raven growled at him as Thomi winced.

"This will be a fight to the death!" the goblin mage shouted. "To the winner goes the morsel!" he added laughing, gesturing at the glaring Se'and.

The ogre glared at the self-styled Lord of Niota. The goblin smiled and uttered an elvish word. Stiffening in pain, the ogre bellowed, then the mage pointed at Walsh.

"Beast, kill this creature!"

Raven raced across the pit.

"Walsh! Defend yourself!" Thomi cried as the ogre grimaced and met the beast's charge.

Cle'or had sidled away from Thomi. The audience's attention was completely focused on the scene before them. She drew two throwing daggers and moved to a position directly behind her target. The voice of the elf in her dream whispered to her an idea. Her eyes widened.

Se'and, dangling above the monstrous battle, beat futilely on the bars, gaping at the fight her ward found herself in. "I have to get out of here!"

Something came through the bars and landed beside her. Se'and stared at George's discolored metal dagger. She dared not glance about and draw any attention. Cautiously, she edged toward the knife, then hefted it and moved to pick the cage's lock.

The ogre groaned as Raven's claws cut his arm. He flailed his other arm, striking the beast and sending it toppling end over end. She shook her head as she rose with a scream of rage.

The ogre shambled in a lope toward her, swinging his fists like a mace. Raven ducked then jumped and bit down hard on its heavily muscled bicep. In agony he turned and slammed her to the ground. As she held on with her teeth clamped, the ogre twisted and slammed her again and again.

The crowd cheered. Half dazed, Raven let go and hastened a few steps away. When she came up, the ogre was staring darkly at her, blood streaming from its arm and from the cuts it had taken.

George felt drugged. He blinked, doing his best to move, to concentrate. He fought the haze and found Fri'il seated at his side. She straightened, "Thank the Lords! We thought we had lost you! You've been fevered for days!"

"Fevered?" he mumbled. He mentally reached out for rapport and didn't find it. His computer staff was originally intended as a tool, an extension of his mind, but since falling into this world it felt more like it was the other half of himself. Without it, he felt incomplete.

She brought a drink brought to his lips. He shook his head violently, spilling it all.

"Oh, my, look what you've done?" She dabbed at the spill, then bent and kissed him passionately.

Something was very wrong. He turned his head away violently. "Why can't I move my arms and legs?"

Crestfallen, Fri'il backed away filled with despair. Tears filled her eyes.

"You had to be bound for your own safety," she muttered as she disgustedly removed her livery and drew her knife while tears streamed down her cheeks.

As he stared, she put the knife to her bodice strings and sliced them open, leaving her bosom bared.

"Am I so ugly? Why can't you love me as a Lord of Cathart ought?"

"Fri'il," he muttered, feeling nauseous, "cut my bindings!"

She shook her head, her eyes glazed. The knife in her hands gleamed in the light. She turned it toward him.

"Why can't you love me?"

Cle'or waited just long enough to see Se'and pick the lock and slip out to drop into the pit.

Raslinn muttered a word as he heard the faintest sound of warning and saw Se'and's escape. He turned in a blur and caught the thrown dagger from the stands and yelled.

"Guards! Guards!"

Raven spun on her heels as Se'and landed on her back and brought the odd blade down on the collar. It instantly sizzled then burst apart as Raven dodged aside. She then leapt forward and shimmered into bird form.

The goblin mage stared in disbelief, "No!" He dove forward and grabbed something obscured as a blast of supernatural energy shot unerringly toward the freed were.

The ogre stared, then raised a thick fist to slam the new intruder when he heard Thomi cry, "No, Walsh! They're friends!"

Cle'or drew her sword and fought back two of the guards. She cursed as Raven was knocked from the air. Other guards raced around the circumference of the pit as pandemonium broke out among spectators eager to flee. Cle'or dispatched her first opponent then cast a dagger underhanded at the second.

Raslinn turned and stared, "Another Cathartan. Quite impressive. Now, kill her!"

The remaining guards were nearly upon her then one cried out having a sudden seizure. The goblin turned as a second cried out. Balfour stood in the main entry his hand upraised, sweat beading his brow as he stared at the falling guards.

The goblin gaped, having felt no magery being wielded. He heard a squawk and narrowly dove aside as Raven returned to the attack. A thick hand clasped the edge of the pit before him and the goblin paled.

The ogre's other hand got purchase. The goblin hastily fled.

Se'and caught the rope that Mc'oh and the woman who had previously tenanted the pit threw down to her. Raven shimmered and returned to beast form, then raced after the retreating goblin as the ogre reached the stands.

"Ras-linn!" he shouted as Thomi raced after him.

"Where are Je'orj and Fri'il?" Se'and shouted.

Me'oh shrugged, "We didn't see them on our way here!"

Thomi's mother said, "I know where your friends are."

Balfour and Cle'or reached them as they rushed from the chamber.

"Fri'il, free me from these bounds!" he muttered, struggling against the cords that bound his wrists and ankles, suddenly feeling the haze lift around him.

She looked back on him wanly, holding the knife threateningly. "Why won't you love me? I will bear you strong daughters!"

"Release me and we can talk about it!" he said with some concern.

Then the door was flung wide and George stared in shock as a figure occupied the doorway. Staff was pulsing darkly in the being's hand.

"You're awake? I would have thought she would have dosed you insensate by now."

"A goblin? You are certainly far from home." He concentrated and tried to link with the staff, yet nothing seemed to happen for a moment.

'Geo-rge, he-lp me.'

The goblin mage smiled thinly and breathed rapidly. Something momentarily wrung the breath from him. He slammed the door firmly shut then barred it behind him.

"No matter, perhaps it will be better this way with you awake and knowing you have brought this doom upon yourself."

"Why don't you love me?" Fri'il rasped inconsolably as the goblin laughed.

George looked at her as she brandished the knife. "Fri'il, it is not a matter of love. I cannot do this. I must return to my world."

"Hear that, my dear," Raslinn practically cackled in delight. "He will not sire the children you must bear to secure your house. He means to betray you! He has always meant to!"

"You must love me!" she pleaded. "Your life is here with us!" She gestured at her bosom. "Am I not pleasing enough?"

George swallowed hard, wondering how he could make her understand that he could not accept what she offered. He had to go home. This was not his world. This place had no right to just summon him and thrust him into a fate he could never have imagined.

"I can't..." he muttered in frustration.

She slumped forward sobbing and the goblin mage laughed.

"So the augury has foretold!" He began to sing the spell chant and the staff flared with dark energy.

'George!' screamed the computer staff, distantly.

He blinked and saw a stygian blackness well from the staff. It was death personified, born of the goblin's maniacal hatred and Fri'il's heart-wrenching, innocent agony. It reached out toward the knife in Fri'il's hands. The darkness touched it and she rose stiffly, a dread anger blazing in her eyes.

With a sigh, George closed his eyes and said, "Fri'il, I do love you."

Her eyes widened and her hands trembled as the goblin mage gasped, "That's a lie! You know in your heart he will never give you what you most desire! He kills your house aborning!"

Yet deep within her George's words echoed, 'love you,' and they awoke the power of her duty.

"Kill him!" the goblin cried.

Fri'il's hands trembled, though she made no move to obey.

Furious, Raslinn screamed, "So be it, then!" He raised the staff over his head and chanted to the stygian emptiness that lay growing on the blade.

The darkness inched up her arms. It would have a soul just as the goblin had promised.

The ogre took the stairs several at a time knocking aside several guards. Raven howled as she reached the doorway with the unmistakable scent of the goblin. She struck the door with her shoulder, only to be cast backward as the warding flared, rebuffing her.

She struck the far wall and shimmered back to human form. The ogre stopped and stared at her, peering down at her. "Me...fought...only...little girl?" he muttered.

Raven shook her head as the ogre offered her his hand and helped her to her feet.

"Need Father's...dagger," Raven explained. "Warded."

The ogre glanced at the door and pounded on it with his right fist. A blast of energy snapped out, stinging his hand. He shook it and grimaced. It had given not the smallest sound of impact. Raven turned and heard running feet. Thomi was only steps ahead of Se'and and the others when the boy paused and stared at her. He blinked, wondering where this naked girl had come from. His mother screeched at him and abruptly covered his eyes.

"Mother!"

Raven shook her head and shouted at Se'and, "Dagger!"

Se'and handed it over and watched Raven run to end of the hall, the ogre curiously following. The unshuttered window was high up and narrow. Putting the dagger between her teeth, Raven gestured for Walsh to help her up. He held out his arms uncertainly. Raven hopped up to take a quick look out the window before scampering onto the ledge.

Thomi caught a brief glimpse of her vanishing back. "Who was that?"

Se'and shook her head, "That is my foster daughter," she said proudly. "Be prepared everyone. It shouldn't be long now."

Cle'or smiled thinly, passing daggers to Balfour and Me'oh, and tossed another to Se'and. "I'm always ready."

Raven moved carefully along the ledge. It had crumbled in places but she was remarkably surefooted even as a human. She listened by the window and could detect nothing. The room was completely warded. She sighed, fearing the worst, then took the knife in her hands and slammed the discolored blade into the shutter. The ward shattered as she threw herself within.

There, the goblin was smiling as Fri'il stiffened and turned the dagger toward her own bared breast, even as the window shattered and a naked form burst across the room.

"The bindings!" his prisoner cried.

A blast of fey energy flicked out from Raslinn's fingertips at the were-child sought to reach the goblin before he could finish chanting his grim spell of death.

210

Raven ducked as the blast struck the wall at the same time that the door behind the mage thudded with a terrific impact, no longer warded against harm, but stout enough to hold for a time.

Raven slashed with her blade at the nearest binding restraining her foster father as she saw the darkness ebb up Fri'il's arms to her shoulders.

Fri'il looked at Raven sadly, "Look after him for me, Raven."

She raised the knife to thrust into her own heart as George shouted, "No!"

White fire flared from the computer staff amid the black energy, and seared the startled goblin's hands.

Fri'il screamed as the blackness flared with opposing white light. She swayed as the dagger began to glow. Raven cut George's other hand free then threw George's dagger with all her might at the goblin.

Raslinn added a word of warding into his chant, which should easily block a thrown blade. His eyes widened as the blade sailed undeterred, then he choked. Uncomprehending, he looked down at the knife sticking from his chest.

The door splintered but still held under the ogre's battering. The ogre redoubled his efforts to break it down at last.

The staff flared pure incandescent white as the goblin mage sank to his knees.

'George!' Staff mentally shouted through their link.

"Je'orj!" Fri'il cried in the distance, lost and far away.

Save her! the Summoning willed. Do what you must!

George's hands trembled as he grabbed at Fri'il's hands as the tip of the blade clove her heart. Blackness welled around them as white flame fought against it.

Blood fountained as George cried, "No!"

Raven stared as the two of them were engulfed in the heatless white flames.

Concentrating, George plucked the knife out and dropped it to the floor as he concentrated and healed Fri'il's gaping wound. He could feel the threads of darkness taking Fri'il's soul as the light burned around them, unable to cast the darkness away.

It fought him while Fri'il fought him out of despair. The darkness was filling her soul. Her heart stopped, her gaze went glassy and she fell slack in his arms.

George heard himself shout, "No! You shall not have her! She is mine!"

He pulled her close and kissed her, breathing life into her as he willed her heart to beat. His breath poured into her stilled lungs, then he drew back and took another deep breath.

"Breathe, Fri'il!" He felt no return of his resuscitation. She lay lifeless in his arms, bathed in light. He kissed her again and again in silence.

Moments passed that seemed a lifetime. He felt her heart beat gently and she gasped a breath and inhaled. Her eyes opened wide and glowed with white fire. Her arms went around him and the darkness fled from her spirit in anathema.

Raven gaped as the darkness flowed to the floor, then pooled around the dying goblin. Raslinn stirred and gasped in horror as it claimed the soul of the one who summoned it and vanished, Raslinn with it.

Staff blazed, its light reflected in George's eyes as he held Fri'il close. She blinked, then returned his kiss and in delight knocked him backward on the bed.

The bar to the door shattered and Se'and and Cle'or quickly edged past the tiring ogre. Raven shook her head at the gaping faces, and picked up Fri'il's fallen dagger to cut the final binding from her oblivious foster father's leg.

"Mmmm," "Hmmm," the unintended audience heard as they stared at the sudden lovers.

Balfour said, "Ahem, well, there must be someone around here who can use a healer, so if you'll excuse me."

Me'oh chuckled as she followed him.

"Well, Se'and, it looks like we've got ourselves a proper Cathartan lord," Cle'or muttered.

"Uh-hmm," she replied as Raven looked up and saw Thomi's mother hastily covering her son's eyes yet again.

In the fortress's courtyard, Se'and confronted the prisoners, which offered her a much needed distraction, uncertain about how she was feeling. It was what she wanted, wasn't it?

The surviving Niota guards were all old men, who blinked at her as if waking up from a dream. She knew that she had fought young vigorous men, but obviously Raslinn had been a truly powerful weaver of illusion.

The whole keep was in shambles. She listened half-heartedly as Thomi told the raggedly dressed refugees that Raslinn was dead.

"He will haunt our lives no more!"

"But what are we to do now?" a woman asked.

Thomi sighed as Walsh ambled to his side. "We have a choice. We came here for refuge. We can either stay or go back where we came from."

Balfour came over and said, "I would not advise returning to the Crescent Lands. Fenn du Blain controls both Gwed and Trelor. His people are raiding the lands below."

The crowed greeted the news with horror. Thomi put his hand on Walsh's now healed arm and said, "Then we stay."

"But this is Imperial land, the elvin lords rule!" a man shouted.

Walsh growled, "Thomi lord here!"

Thomi looked up at his friend in surprise.

No one chose to argue, however, and the ogre smiled.

Cle'or watched the scene with interest as Walsh turned around as if listening to something.

Wonderful, Cle'or thought, *I hear an exultantly laughing old elf everywhere I go. I wonder what he's hearing?*

The ogre was nodding thoughtfully. "Thomi...Lord Niota." He bent and bowed to the boy.

Raven curled up licking her paws at the top of the stairs that led to the guestroom. Bright white light shone through the edge of the blanket that now served as the room's door. She paused, trying to decide if there was any danger in the sounds coming from the bright room but decided to heed Cle'or's warning not to interfere.

She shook her head and hoped that if this was any indication of what might happen when she found a mate, she would not have to scream so.

"Father?" his daughter muttered beside him as she sensed him stir. "Father?"

The aged elf lay in a cocoon of darkness, which was keeping him alive, only moments from death.

Highmage Alrex felt his Summoning exult. It offered him only glimpses of what it learned. The man was in the Empire, at long last, and fate was binding him to this world whether he willed it or no.

And apparently the man was quite stubborn, which might actually help him survive what was to come. He only hoped the man would live to reach him. The Empire was not for the faint of heart, particularly not for a human, even when that human was obviously a mage of great power and skill.

"Father?"

"Wina," he muttered ever so faintly.

"Father!"

"Listen, Wina. He comes."

"What? Who comes?"

So much he needed to say but could not. But this? How could a father not tell his daughter this?

"Bal-four," he whispered before he husbanded what life he had remaining.

Carwina gasped. Her father said no more. He didn't need to. She rose and stalked out of the room. The servants fled as she began breaking things with abandon.

Continued in *Merchants and Mages,* Book 2 of *Highmage's Plight*

A special offer to readers of this book…

- Imagine getting an advance look at another book or story in this series.
- Imagine one day being able to be an exclusive character in the series, serving as the spirit of the character, advising on the character's dialogue or actions, with approval of the author.

Welcome to Highmage's Plight/Dhr2believe.net Group, where the Highmage's plight can become your own!

Highmage's Plight is different from tradition books in that the Plight is intended to evolve over time online. A limited number of readers with the purchase of this book have the opportunity to join what is essentially an experiment.

To learn about the current promotion, allowing a select number of readers to join the Highmage's Plight/Dhr2believe Group, visit www.dhr2believe.net and use the word "Cathartan" when seeking to participate.

Author Biography

D.H. Aire has walked the ramparts of the Old City of Jerusalem and through an escape tunnel out of a Crusader fortress that Richard the Lionheart once called home. He's toured archeological sites that were hundreds, if not thousands of years old... experiences that have found expression in his writing of his Highmage's Plight Series. D.H. Aire's short stories and a serialized version of Highmage's Plight have been featured in the ezine Separate Worlds and appears in their first anthology, *Flights of Fantasy, Vol. 1* (available on Smashwords.com). Other books in the series include: *Merchants and Mages, Human Mage, Highmage,* and, in the shortly to be released, *Well Armed Brides.*

Sample chapters of the first book in his new series, *Dare 2 Believe* are available on Wattpad.com. *Dare 2 Believe* has a tentative publication date of Spring 2015.

The author is originally from St. Louis, Missouri and currently resides in the Washington D.C. metropolitan area. He has an active support site for his story at www.dhr2believe.net.

Caliburn Books presents the high fantasy story The Imundari Hunt:

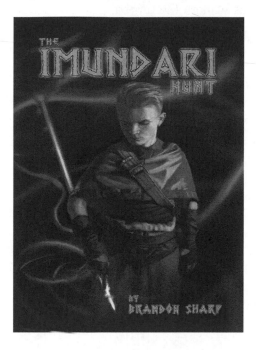

Cody and his new-found acquaintance, Amber, are sucked through a portal through time and space to the magical world of Ortona. In Ortona human teenagers are magically powerful warriors that wield arcane rings, rings which turn into personalized weapons. Very quickly Cody and Amber realize that nearly everything in Ortona is dangerous and trying to kill them. As *The Imundari Hunt* unfolds, come to battle another rare and strange creature, the gray demon which hunts the humans of Ortona.

All humans want to see the demon die, but how far are they willing to go to get the task done? The young orphaned earthlings must pull together and unite with bonds of new friendship and loyalty, things they had never learned to develop on Earth. The journey requires Cody, Amber, and their friends to rely on their skills and a whole lot of luck. Will they pass the test? Will they be strong enough to defeat the demon?

Made in the USA
Middletown, DE
02 June 2015